FIRE OF THE DREKI

THE SERGONES COVEN

L.E. WILSON

RD,
Don't be afraid of the fire inside you.

Much love,
L.E. Wilson
RJR 2018

EVERBLOOD
PUBLISHING

ALSO BY L.E. WILSON

Deathless Night Series (The Vampires)

Blood Hunger

Blood Vengeance

Blood Obsession

Blood Betrayal

Blood Submission

Blood Choice

The Kincaid Werewolves (The Werewolves)

To Covet The Fae

Fae Encounter

Fae Hunter

Copyright © 2018 by Everblood Publishing

All rights reserved. No part of this publication may be reproduced, distributed, or transmitted in any form or by any means, including photocopying, recording, or other electronic or mechanical methods, without the prior written permission of the publisher, except in the case of brief quotations embodied in critical reviews and certain other noncommercial uses permitted by copyright law. For permission requests, email the publisher, addressed "Attention: Permissions Coordinator," at the address below.

All characters and events in this book are fictitious. Any resemblance to actual persons – living or dead – is purely coincidental.

le@lewilsonauthor.com

Paperback Edition ISBN: 978-1-945499-18-0

Publication Date: October 11, 2018

Editor: Jinxie Gervasio @ jinxiesworld.com

Cover Design: Wicked Smart Designs

Cover Photo: Wander Aguiar Photography

Front Cover Model: Jonny James

Back Cover Model: Stock Photo, Deposit Photo

CHAPTER 1

The first time Kohl saw her was months ago on the news as she was escorted into a courtroom surrounded by lawyers. Journalists shoved cameras and microphones in her face, all trying to get a glimpse of her expression for the sole purpose of giving the people at home a thrill at the expense of someone else's pain.

A softer, more innocent version of the woman she was now.

The second time he saw her, she was dancing alone in the corner of the dimly lit club where he worked, body grinding to the dark pulse of the music as though no one else was there. And as far as he was concerned, no one was. The soft innocence that once cloaked her was gone, and in its place was the cold harshness of the reality of this world, and the people in it.

Her name was Devon Young.

A black dress hugged her tall form from her elegant throat to the tops of the combat boots on her feet, covering her tawny skin, as though she were trying to blend into the shadows.

As if she possibly could.

Her hair was different. Darker. Longer. Curlier. More natural. The curls floated around her head in time to her movements with a life all their own, hiding her from him. But Kohl didn't need to see her face. He knew exactly what she looked like.

The song pumping through the speakers hit its crescendo, and Kohl's blood pulsed in time to the heavy bass. Each hit of the drum reverberated through his muscles until his bones vibrated and his upper lip twitched, his fangs tasting the air, the music and the erotic motions of her body working together to rattle the tenacious hold he had on his control. Music always affected him like this. The lure of it. The power of it.

But tonight it was worse. Because tonight, *she* was here.

Kohl turned his back on the crowd of humans huddled around the bar, hiding the telltale signs of what he truly was, and started washing dirty glasses, letting Andrew handle the drink orders. He needed a minute to give himself time to regain control of his body's errant reaction. Though he didn't always bartend, they were short-handed tonight, so he'd offered to pitch in and help. It was the least he could do for the vampires who had taken him in when he'd had no one and nowhere else to go.

As he washed glasses and refilled garnishes, the repetitive actions soothed the fire in his blood, and his mind wandered back to the human woman. What was she doing there? Just outside of San Antonio, Texas, of all places? He thought she lived in Dallas. And how did she get in? The club his adopted family owned didn't exactly advertise its existence. As a matter of fact, entry was strictly enforced and by invitation only—by a member of the coven or one of their trusted human pets. Which meant she'd have to know someone who was a regular guest, and no one had ever mentioned her.

The faces of every human who'd ever walked through the door flashed through his mind, their image forever engraved in his memory. None of them were at her level. None of them deserved a woman like Devon.

He'd never met her, yet he *knew* her.

Even now, if he closed his eyes, he could smell her...feel her. Her anger. Her shame. Her longing.

Her weariness with it all.

Kohl felt it, and understood it. For he often experienced those same emotions himself. He was familiar with the weight she carried.

Devon's scent suddenly grew stronger, overtaking the smell of alcohol and cheap cologne, and he knew she was there at the bar. Grinding his teeth against the temptation she posed, he set down the glass he was drying and turned around, unable to resist the chance to interact with her.

"I got this," he told Andrew.

His friend and co-worker gave him a sharp look, his dark eyes quickly assessing Kohl's appearance before he nodded and went back to his own side of the bar.

She stood between two other human females who'd been waiting for a while. His heart hammering in a way that had nothing to do with the song pounding out of the speakers, Kohl indicated he'd be right with her and took their orders first. Once he got them out of the way, he braced himself and smiled.

"Sorry about that. What can I do for you?" He had to shout over the music for her to hear him.

Her eyes—an intriguing mixture of brown and gold with the slightest upward tilt at the outer corners—met his for a moment before traveling over the tattoos on his neck. At least, the visible ones. His skin heated everywhere they touched, and he wished he could hear what she was thinking, but unlike the others, he lacked that ability. A genetic defect.

A small diamond glittered on the right side of her nose. It was the only jewelry she wore. She returned his smile, but it didn't reach those beautiful eyes. "Can you distort time and space and send me back a few years?"

Her words, spoken in low tones not really meant to be overheard, came to him clear enough, and his stomach fell as Kohl felt her mood take a sudden dive. His smile faltered. He knew her request had nothing to do with her age—no older than thirty—and everything to do with what had happened to her following that night on the news. "No, I'm afraid I can't."

She looked down at her fingers, twisted together on the bar, unsurprised he had heard her over the music and chatter. It was a moment before she raised her chin. "You know who I am, don't you?" Then she laughed a little, glancing off to the side. She flushed, spots of dark red marring the flawless brown skin on her neck and chest. "Of course, you do. Everyone does. Even way the fuck out here."

As she'd already answered her own question, Kohl didn't bother to respond. "Can I get you something to drink... Devon?" He kept his eyes on her face, away from the rush of blood under that soft-looking skin, so close to the surface it would only take the slightest nick of a fang to release it.

She raised her voice. "Vodka and cranberry juice would be great, thank you. Heavy on the vodka." Abruptly, she turned her back to him and leaned back against the bar to watch the dancers.

Dismissed, Kohl wondered what he'd said or done to cause her to shut down the way she had. The entire state knew who she was, if not the entire country. It shouldn't surprise her that he did also. Whatever was bothering her, her emotions were all over the place, wreaking havoc on his calm façade, so he set about making her drink for her and set it on the bar.

His eyes travelled over the disarray of curls that covered the back of her head. Without thinking, he lifted his hand to touch them before remembering himself and letting it fall. Picking up a towel, he made a show of drying his hands. "It's on the house," he told her.

She turned with a negative shake of those curls. "That's not necessary. I can pay."

"I know you can pay. But, it's on me. Really." He wanted to do something to apologize, even though he didn't know how he'd offended her.

After a slight hesitation, she took the drink and met his eyes. "Thank you…uh…"

His hands stilled on the towel. "Kohl. My name is Kohl. Kohl Sergones."

"Kohl." She tasted the name on her tongue as she eyed up the ink on the back of his hands and arms, revealed beneath the rolled up sleeves of his white dress shirt, then moved up to the black tie strangling his throat. "Aren't you guys a little dressed up for such a grungy place?"

Unconsciously, he ran a hand over the front of his shirt, smoothing out invisible wrinkles. "It's what's required." When he looked up again, she was watching him with a glint of light in her eyes. The heaviness of her emotions shifted a little, and he realized she was teasing him. He smiled and shrugged. "I guess it makes it easy to tell the clientele apart from the staff."

"Well, it does at that." She lifted her drink in a half-hearted salute. "Thank you, Kohl."

"You're welcome, Devon."

He watched her walk back to her corner, weaving in and out of the other humans, hips swaying with a rhythm that was both seductive and totally unconscious. She had to feel his lingering attention, but she didn't look back. Slugging down half of the contents in her glass, she joined the other dancers.

Kohl slowly exhaled and turned his attention to his waiting customers. But as he poured shots, shook Cosmos, and topped off glasses of beer, her words tumbled around in his head. Why did she assume he thought she couldn't pay for her drinks?

Admittedly, he didn't know what had happened to her after the trial. Perhaps she'd lost her job. Perhaps she was dependent on others.

Which led him back around to wondering how she was able to get into the club. She had to know someone here. Or, perhaps one of the other vampires had already claimed her, and he hadn't realized because he'd only just tonight caught her scent. He squeezed his eyes shut against the red haze of an unforeseen rage. The glass he held shattered in his hand.

Andrew shot him a look and grabbed the broom.

Kohl shook his head slightly, trying to clear it of the woman. He had no right to feel this way about her, and didn't know why he was obsessing over her, or why he'd been doing it since that day he'd seen her on the evening news.

Maybe "obsessing" wasn't the right word. It made him sound like a stalker. But he certainly hadn't forgotten her. Little everyday things would often bring her to mind, and he'd found himself wondering what had happened to her after the trial more times than he could count. And then, tonight, she'd shown up out of the blue, like he'd somehow conjured her himself with some sort of black magic born from his longing not to be alone.

A movement at the edge of the dance floor caught his eye, and was gone just as quickly. At first he saw nothing out of the ordinary, just humans grinding lewdly against each other, hyped up on alcohol and vampire blood, attempting to ease the loneliness of their short lives. But Kohl knew this place like the back of his hand. Something wasn't right.

He signaled to Andrew and wandered over to the far end of the bar, less crowded now, and searched for whatever it was that had raised a flag. A second later, the flash of the strobe lights glinted off a shiny, black barrel. And then again on the other side of the club. Human eyes wouldn't have caught it, but Kohl had a…gift…of eyesight, if one could call it that. And he knew immediately what he had seen.

Before the first shooter had a chance to squeeze the trigger, he was over the bar and across the room, his only thought being to protect Devon. Fire razed his hip, and he hissed in pain as a bullet seared through the muscle and out the other side, just missing the bone. He barely flinched. His focus centered on getting to the woman. To Devon.

He was at her side before the sounds of gunshots registered to the dancers over the music. Without pause, Kohl tackled her to the floor, yelling at her to stay down when bodies began falling around them. Then he tucked her beneath his body and crawled over to one of the sitting areas, dragging her with him. She was tall for a woman, easily five ten or so, but with his size, he covered her easily.

Flipping one of the round tables over and using it as a shield, he barricaded them in the corner. The tabletop was made of armored steel, to be used specifically for this purpose. Devon huddled behind it with her knees pulled up to her chest and her hands covering her ears as people screamed and ran over each other, trying to get to the exits to avoid the barrage of firepower exploding from the rifle barrels. Bullets ricocheted around them, and he pushed her head down, both to keep her safe and to keep her from seeing exactly what it was that was trying to protect her.

The beast inside Kohl stirred and woke. The one he tried so hard to suppress. It was bad enough his fangs were exposed and aching to tear through flesh. He didn't need to fight the beast, too. But try as he might to resist it, his blood burned hot as blue fire, and his skin felt simultaneously loose and tight as chaos exploded around them.

The smell of human blood filled his nostrils, feeding his hunger. He wanted to help the other victims, but to try and do so would expose him for what he was, would expose all of them. It was bad enough he'd just sprinted from one side of the club to the other in a second's time or less. The place was small, but it wasn't that small. He could only hope the shooters were enough of a distraction that no one had caught him on their phone cameras as anything more than a blur, if it managed to pick him up at all.

More gunfire came on the scene, short pops muffled by silencers only vampires would be able to distinguish among the screams and music, and he knew the club's owners had arrived. The shooters didn't stand a chance. He just had to wait it out. Wrapping his arms around Devon, he hunched over her trembling form, protecting her as much as he could with his body.

Her scent filled his lungs, different now, tinged with the fear and horror that kept her frozen beneath him. Kohl shivered, his throat burning and his fangs straining with delight at the prospect of her taste. But he clamped down on his instincts, maintaining control on his hunger, concentrating on keeping the beast at bay.

When it was all over, the sudden silence was nearly as deafening to him as the chaos had been moments before. Voices came to his ears, speaking in low tones. Voices he knew well. And he moved the table out of the way so he could stand.

Four vampires surveyed the results of the shooting, guns at their sides, checking the bodies for life. The gore didn't faze them. One or two of them had done much worse during a casual night out on the town.

Bending down, Kohl touched Devon lightly on the back, gently trying to soothe her trembling. "It's finished, Devon. It's all clear. Here,"—he slid his hand down her arm— "let me help you up." He knew by staying near her she would see him as he was, but there was no avoiding it. He couldn't just run away and leave her to the mercy of the coven. The Master wouldn't care what was done with her. But Kohl did, and he needed to make sure she got out of there all in one piece.

Devon took his proffered hand and allowed him to haul her to her feet. Her eyes shot from one bloody body to the next, then to the holes in the walls and the overturned tables and chairs, taking in the destruction around them with wide eyes. "Oh, my God."

Someone turned off the music and flicked on the lights

behind the bar, and Kohl quickly turned his face away, hiding in the shadows.

She touched him on the forearm, her fingers digging into his skin. "Thank you." Her voice shook, and she cleared her throat. "Thank you for protecting me. Or I'd probably be lying..." He heard a sob catch in her throat.

His skin tingled where she touched him. Covering his fangs with his lips, ignoring the prick of pain as the points jabbed into the soft flesh of his mouth, he covered her hand with his and gave her a nod.

Devon zeroed in on his eyes, her tears abating by the distraction. She became very still, her full lips parted on a quick inhale.

Fuck. His eyes. He'd forgotten about his eyes.

"Kohl."

Hawke, the coven's second oldest vampire, handed his pistol to one of the bouncers and came walking toward them, pushing his dark hair off his forehead. In spite of his age, his physical appearance was that of a man in the prime of his life.

His expression was grim as he reached out a hand to introduce himself to Devon. "Hello…" He let his sentence trail off, and looked at her expectantly.

She blinked and released Kohl's arm, her attention successfully averted. "Devon," she said. Her voice still shook, but only slightly. "My name is Devon."

"Devon," Hawke repeated. "What a lovely name. I'm Hawke. Are you hurt?"

Kohl quickly scanned her body, looking for injuries. He hadn't even thought to check. She could be in shock. Her dress was dusty from the floor, but otherwise she appeared unharmed.

"No, I seem to be fine. Thanks to Kohl." Her eyes lingered for a moment too long on his face before she turned back to Hawke.

He wished she wouldn't study him like that. He had a feeling she saw way too much. Much more than his physical appearance.

Hawke snapped his fingers, and Andrew came forward.

"Please call Devon a cab and see that she gets *safely* into it."

"I have my car—" she began.

"I'll have it returned to you tomorrow. I don't think you should be driving after such a traumatizing evening."

"But, what about the police? Don't I need to stay to give a statement? I think I got a pretty good look at one of the shooters."

"The shooters are dead now." Hawke swung his arm in a wide circle, taking in the pile of bodies leaking all over the floor. "As are most of our patrons, unfortunately." He caught both of Devon's hands in his, effectively capturing her attention again.

Kohl's eyes fell to their joined hands and he exposed his fangs with a hiss. Hawke was his friend, but he didn't like him touching her.

Hawke's eyes flicked over to him before returning to Devon's face, and he released her hands. "Let us get you safely home. It'll ease my mind after all that's happened tonight. We'll handle the police. If anyone asks, just say you left before this all went down. There's no need for you to be involved."

Even though he'd let go of her hands, Hawke held her eyes with his, extending his influence over her just enough to keep her calm and get her to do what he wanted. Kohl clenched his teeth. He'd witnessed this game before, and he knew it was necessary, but he didn't like him in her head any more than he liked him touching her.

Her eyes glazed over. "Okay," she agreed amiably.

Hawke waved Andrew forward. He was already on his phone, calling for a driver.

Though the fire in his blood had cooled somewhat, Kohl was still fighting the effects of the heavy scent of blood. More so than the others. It was a never-ending battle for him.

He needed some air.

"Will you walk me out?"

He looked down at Devon, surprised by her request, then over at Hawke.

His friend took in his appearance, assessing where his head was, and gave Kohl a nod. "Help Andrew see her off. We'll talk after."

"I'll be right back," Kohl said. Placing his hand on Devon's lower back, he escorted her around the ones who had fallen and out the back door. She obediently went with him, barely glancing at the gore around her.

The night was dark, but the motion light lit up a twenty-foot perimeter. Kohl didn't need it, but proper lighting was an integral part of the illusion of the club. He peered into the shadows and smelled the air, assuring they were alone before he let Devon join him outside and allowed the door to shut behind them. The human's New Year had just passed, and it was actually pretty cold for central Texas. The bare branches of oak trees reached toward the dark sky with skeletal fingers, their trunks kept warm by the smaller cypress and cedars. The grass was dead and straw-like, interspersed with clumps of prickly pear cactus.

Devon walked past him, then stopped and spun around.

Calm radiated from her. Hawke's influence. And for once, Kohl was glad of his interference.

"No cops are coming, are they?"

Kohl saw no reason to lie to her. She wouldn't remember this conversation. He was one hundred percent positive Andrew was going to wipe her memories of this night before he put her in the cab. "No."

She took the news with an air of composure. It didn't surprise him as much as her next move.

Reaching up, she touched the corner of his mouth with her fingertips, near his fang. Then let her fingertips trail through the short hairs of his beard.

His upper lip twitched from her touch and he barely managed to repress the sound of pleasure her touch wrought. Kohl held perfectly still, unsure where she was going with this, but enjoying the nearness of her too much to stop her.

"What are you, Kohl?"

Again, there was no reason to outright lie. He knew she was one of the few humans in the world who were aware of creatures like him. It was the reason she had been in that courtroom.

Well, maybe not exactly like him.

"I'm…" He paused, rethinking his answer. "Different." He'd very nearly revealed everything, but something stopped him at the last moment.

"I bet you are."

The words were said in a light tone he knew was meant to be flirty, but there was still a trace of wonder there. Again, he wished he could read her thoughts.

The door opened behind Kohl, and Andrew joined them.

"Your cab is on its way," he told Devon.

Her hand fell from Kohl's face. She crossed her arms against the cold and thanked him. With a hint of a hesitant smile, she dropped her chin and kicked at a small stone stuck in the dirt.

Kohl felt the air rush from his lungs when her touch left him. "Andrew, give us a second, will you?"

"Hawke told me to make sure she got in the cab okay," he said.

"She will. I just want a minute. Please."

After a brief hesitation, Andrew gave him a nod. "I'll be right inside. Just let me know when it gets here."

"Thanks, man."

"Sure thing."

Kohl knew the only reason he was agreeing was because whatever happened between him and Devon, she wouldn't remember. And so it wouldn't become an issue.

The door closed behind Andrew, and Kohl suddenly found he had no idea what to say to her. But he wanted to say something, even if she wouldn't remember it, something that would distract her from the horrors of the evening. "I saw you on the news," he blurted. "That's how I knew who you were." As soon as the words were out of his mouth, he wished he could take them back. Reminding her of a separate traumatic event wasn't exactly what he'd been going for.

But she took it in stride. "I assumed," she told him. "So, what's with the eyes? I mean, they're back to brown now, but earlier they were way lighter, and the pupils—"

He cut her off. "It was nothing, Devon." Stepping closer, he noticed the way his heartbeat became much more pronounced and the warmth returned to his blood in response to being near her. He stopped just short of touching her, lest it got to be too much too soon. For some reason, this woman brought out the beast in him. Quite literally. "Look, I just wanted..." He searched her face, but the words wouldn't come. So, he retreated again, placing one hand on the opposite shoulder as he scanned the trees behind her. He sighed heavily. "I don't really know what I wanted."

She observed his behavior with a lack of emotion that was a bit disconcerting coming from a human, even though he knew why she was so calm. And, he was glad Hawke had saved her from the horrors she'd just witnessed.

He crossed his arms over his chest, mimicking her stance. "I just wanted to make sure you're all right."

"Are you afraid of me?" she asked.

Something between a laugh and a snort came out of his mouth. "No. Why would I be afraid of you?" His eyes fell from her face, to her full chest and rounded hips, and back again. She was easily half his size. And human.

"I have no idea. Except your body language tells me otherwise."

"So...what? You're some kind of expert?"

"I don't have to be. Though I did take some classes in college." She nodded at his arms, still crossed in front of him. "You keep crossing your body with your arms, like you're trying to force me to keep my distance. Which, by the way, is completely uncalled for, since it's *you* who keeps coming at *me*."

"I can't seem to help it," he told her honestly. Then he nodded at her own arms, crossed tightly across her body. "And it appears I'm not the only one."

That shut her up fast, but only for a few seconds. "Why did you save me, Kohl?"

There was something in her tone, something he didn't like

hearing. Like she almost wished he hadn't bothered. "I don't know, but I'm glad I did."

Again with the honesty. Following her lead from before, he left one arm across his chest and reached out with the other to touch the corner of her mouth with his fingertips. He ran his thumb over her lower lip. It was full and soft. Softer than he'd imagined.

He had the sudden urge to take it between his teeth.

Her heart stuttered at his touch, then began to race, pounding loudly in his ears. The beast stirred within him again, and he told himself he needed to stop...

Lights swung across them as the cab pulled up and parked at the end of the building. Kohl dropped his arm and stepped back. Without taking his eyes from her face, he rapped on the back door. "Cab's here."

"Kohl—" Devon reached for him, eyes wide with panic.

"It's okay," he told her. "It'll be okay. Goodbye, Devon." As Andrew came out, he turned away and stepped inside, pulling the door shut firmly behind him.

Alone, he braced his back against the cold metal and concentrated on breathing.

Fuck.

CHAPTER 2

Devon woke the next morning to the loud patter of a surprise Texas hailstorm hitting the roof. It matched the pounding in her head. With a groan, she sat up and pressed the heels of her hands against her temples. Her heart was racing. The storm must have startled her from sleep.

What the hell had been in those drinks last night?

She remembered going out with no specific destination in mind. Just somewhere she could get lost in the music and the darkness and forget her life. Be another nameless person in the crowd. Before she knew it, she'd found herself in front of The Caves. "Exclusive" wasn't quite the word to describe that place. More like "you were never here or we'll have to kill you" was more apt. The owners were a secretive bunch, and she couldn't say she blamed them.

She'd be secretive, too, if the majority of the human race didn't know she existed. And if it weren't for her old job, she'd never know about them, either.

Getting in had been easier than she'd thought it would be. While she'd been sitting in her car, debating whether or not to try her charms on the bouncer—more out of morbid curiosity than anything else—a pickup truck with oversized tires and a pair of balls hanging from its hitch had pulled up alongside her and parked, and a typical Texas good ole' boy had climbed out. With a glance in her direction, he'd plopped his hat on his head and hitched up his Wranglers. Devon had hesitated only for a second before she'd jumped out and caught up to his bowlegged stride, locking her car behind her with the remote. Linking her arm through his, all it took was a smile and a promise for a dance, and she was admitted into the club as his guest.

Once inside, she looked around and couldn't help thinking she fit right in with that crowd. All people like her, dressed in black or similar dark colors to blend in with the shadows, hiding from the rest of the world.

Her cowboy, on the other hand, with his ten-gallon hat, orange patterned shirt, and pointy-toed boots, stuck out like a sore thumb. But that didn't deter him from bellying up to the bar like he owned the place. Devon followed him, ordering a drink from the bartender.

There was only one time she thought they weren't going to allow her to stay, and that was when her date's "friend" showed up. But after the vampire ran his eyes up and down her body in a rather cold, blatant way, causing shivers to chase each other across her skin, he shrugged and told her to have a good time. Then he threw his arm around his cowboy and pulled him away to a dark corner. She didn't see either of them for the rest of the night, but she didn't feel there was cause for concern.

There hadn't been a vampire blamed death recorded for many years.

Besides, she had her own problems.

After they'd left, she remembered dancing for a bit, then going to the bar to order another drink. There was another bartender there helping the first one. One with sweet brown eyes and strong, tattooed forearms. Butterflies had erupted in her stomach when he'd focused all that charisma on her. Just thinking about it now, she had to press her palm to her belly to calm them. He'd known right away who she was. And had given her a drink for free. Not because he'd wanted to fuck her —which would have been her preferred reason, vampire or not —but because he'd pitied her.

God, even the undead felt sorry for her.

Devon barked out an ugly laugh and immediately clamped her palms over her temples to hold her brains in. When she was relatively certain they weren't going to explode from her eye sockets, she rose carefully from her bed, reached over, and closed the blinds that covered her window. She didn't even have to strain herself to get to them. She could cross the entire width of her room in seven steps or less. As a matter of fact, she could walk the length of her entire apartment in about twenty steps. But she didn't mind. It was cozy. It had a great view of downtown Austin. And more importantly, the space was small enough that it made her feel safe.

She came out of the bathroom showered, with her unruly hair pulled back from her face, and dressed in her least-ragged yoga pants and a hoodie, feeling somewhat more human. But when she opened the fridge, she groaned again. There was nothing in there but a few eggs, a near empty jar of salsa, and a container of butter. Her hangover definitely needed something more to soak up the alcohol.

Shutting the door—gently, so as not to disturb her fragile head before the Advil kicked in—she left the refuge of her apartment and knocked on the door across the hall, wincing at the noise.

Frank, her neighbor and only friend in this place, opened it wearing a huge smile on his entirely too handsome face, Superman boxer briefs, and nothing else. He frequently answered his door in this manner of dress—or *undress* as the case may be—but Devon couldn't complain. The guy was in great shape.

"You look terrible." The smile never slipped as he issued his greeting, which also ranged in the "things you never expected" category. At least for those who didn't know him.

She grinned back. "Nothing a tortilla or two won't fix."

He raised his eyes to the ceiling as hail continued to pound the roof. They lived on the top floor of their building, and sometimes it sounded like the weather was coming right through the tiles. "I guess I can't make you go out for your own in this weather. If you make the eggs, I'll bring the tortillas."

"Deal."

"See you in five." And he shut the door in her face.

Devon shook her head. She almost rolled her eyes, but it was entirely too painful to move them. So, she went back to her place to start scrambling up the eggs and salsa. Breakfast Taco Sundays were a thing they'd started shortly after Devon had moved in, after the first time she'd knocked on his door to borrow some tortillas and he'd let her have some as long as he was invited to breakfast. They'd hit it off immediately, and Frank remained her one and only friend in this city. The conversation normally revolved around the latest series on Netflix and the occasional breakdown of the previous night's activities if either of them had happened to brave the singles scene. Or sometimes they watched the latest horror flick (in the morning when the sun was out and the monsters couldn't get them) and hardly spoke at all, but it was nice to have another body in the room either way.

Five minutes later, on the dot, Frank strutted into her apartment, and he'd even had the decency to throw on some lounge pants. "Don't worry, Dev, my love. I have exactly what you need."

"Tortillas?"

"And Ma's famous hangover recipe."

Devon's stomach heaved. "I couldn't possibly drink that stuff again."

"That's what you said last time, but it worked, didn't it?"

"I wouldn't know. My body went into evacuation mode as soon as I choked it down."

"And you felt better, right?"

She had to admit, she had. But she would only ever admit it to herself. Never to Frank. He would tell his mother, and like any good Italian woman, she would immediately take the compliment to mean Devon was the woman who had finally— finally!—managed to capture her only son's heart. His mother had been set on this outcome since the moment she'd laid eyes on the new neighbor when they'd passed in the hallway a few months before. She liked Devon. Enough that she would even overlook the unfortunate fact that Devon's family was originally from Kenya and not even a smidge Italian, though she was convinced there had to be at least a dab of it somewhere in

Devon's ancestry due to the lightness of her skin and her love of pasta.

She also conveniently overlooked the fact that her son was extremely gay.

"So, I actually had a date last night," Frank said as he set the jar of green stuff on the counter.

Devon turned off the stove and grabbed a plate from the cabinet. She glanced over her shoulder as she opened the tortillas. "You did?" she asked with genuine enthusiasm. "How did it go?" Much like her, Frank was a bit of a homebody, and didn't get out much, despite the fact that he looked like a younger, more masculine, yet at the same time prettier, Richard Gere. She was a recluse, too, but she had good reasons. Frank did not.

He shrugged. "Okay, I guess." His eyes widened. "Oh! I almost forgot. When he left this morning, there was some guy lurking around your apartment door. I asked if I could help him. He glared at me and left." He shrugged nonchalantly. "Guess I'm not his type."

Turning with the plate of breakfast tacos in her hand, she frowned at him. "One. I'd say your date was more than okay if he spent the night. And two, who was it?"

"Just a guy I met on the hike and bike trail the other morning when we had that warm day. Thomas? Magnus? Something like that."

She rolled her eyes. "No, dufus. The guy lurking around my door."

He shrugged. "Don't know, my love. Never saw him before. And he wasn't real chatty."

She frowned, trying to place who it could've been, and headed to the small table tucked into the corner of the kitchen, plate of tacos in hand. Frank placed his hand on the small of her back as she passed him to escort her to the table.

Devon immediately stiffened, her feet tripping over each other. Not because he was touching her; Frank was a very touchy guy. But for some reason, the warmth of his hand on her back plucked at something in her brain.

Frank caught the plate before she dropped it. "Hey! Hey! That's my breakfast." Placing it carefully on the table, he frowned at her. "What's up? You okay?"

"Yeah." She shook her head slightly. "Yeah, I'm fine. I just…" She wasn't sure what had just happened. But something about the way he'd just touched her seemed so familiar….

"You should drink The Remedy."

Whatever had been teasing the edge of her memory, it was gone. Devon made a face. "Ugh. Stop talking about it. I'm not drinking it. I just need some food and some more Advil, then I gotta get ready for work."

"But it's Friday. Which is almost Sunday. I thought we could sit around in our underwear and eat unhealthy delivery food we can't afford and binge on Netflix."

"*You* sit around in your underwear. I have the decency to wear clothes. And don't you have to work?"

"Nope. It's a skeleton crew day." He looked so forlorn, she wished she didn't have to. "I wish I could, but I need the cash. Or I won't be able to pay for the subscription."

"We can watch at my place."

Devon laughed. "Surrounded by your creepy doll collection? No thanks."

"They're not creepy. They're porcelain, and antique. You have no appreciation for fine things."

"Still creepy," Devon insisted as they sat down to eat.

Picking up his fork, Frank suddenly got serious. "I don't like you doing the package delivery thing, Dev. It's not safe for a woman alone. You hear stuff all the time about Uber drivers."

"I'll be fine." She took a bite of her taco, chewing carefully around her lingering headache. "I'm only doing a day shift. And I'm not driving murderers around, just packages. The money will tide me over until Mrs. G pays me at the pottery shop."

"You've got way too much up here to be wasting your time on those jobs." He tapped the side of his head with his finger. "You should be the top network security person at these companies, not delivering stuff to their customers."

Her appetite suddenly disappeared, and she dropped her taco onto her plate. "You know I can't do that anymore." She took a drink of water and sat back in her chair. Frank was the only one who knew the whole story.

"Because you need to stand up to that prick."

"Isn't 'prick' a word normally reserved for a guy?"

"Yeah, but in this case, it's totally perfect."

"Frank."

He put his hands up in front of him. "I'm just sayin'."

Devon sighed. "I know. And you're probably right. But at this moment in time I just want to eat my taco, enjoy your company, and go make a little money."

At first she didn't think he was going to let it go, but after a few seconds, he dropped his eyes to his food and picked up his taco. "All right. I'll shut up about it. For now."

"Thank you." Breathing a sigh of relief, she went back to eating, hoping her stomach wouldn't reject the food. She needed the boost in energy. "So, tell me more about this date you had."

"Eh. It wasn't all that."

True to form, he launched into his story of his adventures the night before. But Devon found herself listening with only half an ear. Her mind kept wandering back to the night before, or rather, what she couldn't seem to remember about it. Like getting home, for instance. She never drank so much she couldn't get herself home safely.

After checking that Frank didn't need her to pick up anything for him while she was out, she threw on her largest sunglasses and went out to her car, holding her purse above her head to protect it from the weather, and prayed the painkillers would kick in soon.

Her nondescript tan sedan wasn't in its normal spot in the small parking lot of her apartment complex, and she panicked for a minute, wondering if she'd left it at the club and taken a cab home. She didn't have the money to take another one back to retrieve it, and Frank didn't have a car. Taking the bus wasn't an option, either. They didn't go out that far from the city. Sending up a quick prayer, Devon clicked her remote, listening for the telltale beep, and finally spotted it parked on the street.

She frowned, wondering why the hell she parked her car way over there. Maybe the lot was full when she'd come home? Though this didn't seem likely. The lot was never full. Dodging traffic, she ran across the street. At least she'd remembered to max out the meter.

Shrugging it off, she got in and started the car, turning up the heat. The weather was so finicky this time of year. Luckily, the hail stopped before she reached the warehouse to pick up the packages that needed to go out, and she was able to complete her shift thirty minutes earlier than scheduled. As she'd hoped, the painkillers and food did some good, and Devon thought she might actually feel human enough to brave the grocery store.

But instead, unable to shake the feeling all day that something was…off…she found herself travelling south on I-35.

When she arrived at her destination, she threw her car into park, and stared at the front of The Caves.

CHAPTER 3

THE PREVIOUS NIGHT

"Who was that girl, Kohl?" Hawke was waiting for him when he went back inside after hearing Devon's taxi leave. He sat at the bar with an open bottle of vodka in front of him, spinning slowly back and forth on his stool.

"Devon?" He shrugged. "Just another human who found her way into the club."

Hawke studied him with an unnerving stare as he continued to spin casually back and forth.

His name suits him, Kohl thought, *for he has the sharp eyes of a top predator.*

"Why do I get the feeling there's more to her than that?" he finally asked.

Kohl rubbed the back of his neck, attempting to disperse the sudden heat accumulating there, though he knew Hawke meant her no harm. "She was on the news a few months back. Maybe a year ago? I don't remember. She's the one who spoke up about Parasupe and what they were doing. She even testified against them in court. It was all over the internet."

Hawke's head fell back and he spoke to the ceiling. "Thaaat's right. I thought she looked familiar." He looked back at Kohl. "It wasn't the real story, of course, but what they wanted the general population to believe. And a bunch of online assholes tore her apart for her supposed betrayal to the company. That girl?"

Kohl made a sound of affirmation.

"Everybody's so fucking brave when they're hiding behind their phones and their"—Hawk's mouth twisted with disgust—"*oh-so-cool* social media personas. Get them face to face,"—he flashed his fangs—"and they're pissing their pants."

Kohl walked behind the bar and straightened a few bottles that had fallen over during the shooting. "It was nothing but a fucking witch-hunt, what she went through. I watched the entire thing unfold, as we all did, waiting to see what Parasupe was going to do next. If the general population had the slightest fucking idea what that company really does, they wouldn't be so quick to pick up those torches." Thinking about what he'd just said, he laughed without humor. "Or maybe they'd invest in better weapons and join them." Gauging Hawke's expression, he wondered if he was saying too much, and got the impression that was a very affirmative yes. But he couldn't seem to shut himself up. "Her face was all over the social media sites. Anyone would recognize her if they looked hard enough." A piece of broken glass sliced his finger when he picked it up. It healed before the blood could drip on the floor. He threw the glass in the trash and wiped his hand on his black pants. He was talking too much, showing too much interest in her. He attempted to wrap up the conversation. "Guess she's here in San Antonio now."

"Guess so."

The back of his skull vibrated under Hawke's intense stare. He ignored it for as long as he could. His friend was forever trying to pick the thoughts out of his head, but he never had much luck, even for a vampire of his age. It drove him a little crazy that Kohl was the one person he couldn't read, other than a few vague words or ideas that broke through here and there. But it was also probably why they got along so well.

When he realized Hawke wasn't going to give up any time soon, Kohl turned around and just went ahead and answered the question his friend was trying so hard to glean from his mind. "I don't know her, not personally, just from the news. But she's been through a lot of shit lately. And I just thought getting shot in a nightclub shouldn't be the next thing. That's all." He went back to picking up the broken glass.

"Did it occur to you that maybe she was the reason our club got shot up?" Hawke picked up the bottle of vodka and took a healthy swig before setting it down and wiping his mouth on the sleeve of his pink dress shirt. He always dressed up, and more likely than not in colors other men wouldn't have the balls to wear.

Kohl sighed. Yeah. It *had* occurred to him. And it was only another reason for him to have done what he had.

Hawke caught his gaze with his own. "You can't see her anymore, Kohl."

He knew this. He did. Still, the words hit him hard. "I know."

He thought Hawke was gonna keep on him about it, but he didn't. With one last pensive look, the vampire went to go "talk" to the cleaning crew who had just arrived. They wouldn't remember the job, but they would be paid well. Their families taken care of. It was how Hawke worked.

Andrew joined Kohl behind the bar with a broom and a mop to help him clean up. His short, dark hair, spiked every which way with dried gel, hadn't moved an inch. "You doin' okay?"

"Yeah. I'm good." He took the dustpan from him and held it so Andrew could sweep the broken glass into it.

"These guys weren't your ordinary good ole' boy nut jobs," Andrew said. "They picked this place, and knew how to get the weapons inside without us finding them."

"Do we know who they were?"

"Not yet. The ones who were inside tearing up the place are all dead, and there wasn't anything on the bodies to identify them. But we're gonna look for the driver tomorrow night."

"The driver? What driver?"

Andrew leaned the broom against the wall and got the mop as Kohl emptied the dustpan. They didn't need to be doing this, that's what the cleaning crew was for, but they did it anyway. Having a bunch of guys come in and shoot your clientele all to hell was enough to make anyone restless.

"There was a driver waiting outside. He took off before we could catch him."

"Did Mark catch the plate numbers? He was working the door last night, right?"

"Yeah, he was. But no, he didn't see anything. He came running inside as soon as they started shooting, and by the time he went back outside, the car was leaving. It didn't have any plates. They must've taken them off before they came here."

"Smart."

"Yup."

Kohl's head was all over the place. If the driver was still out there, and they *had* come here to take out Devon, then that meant they would go after her again as soon as they regrouped. His insides roiled in protest, stirring the beast.

"Kohl, whatever's bugging you, you need to chill."

He looked up to find Andrew watching him warily. "I'm tight."

"Your eyes are telling me something different."

Rubbing the back of his neck to ease the burning tension there, Kohl closed his eyes and took a few deep breaths. When he opened them again, Andrew gave him a nod and went back to work.

"Is anyone going to go check on the girl? On Devon?"

Andrew shrugged. "Not that I'm aware of. You know how the Master is. He doesn't give a shit about humans other than the money and feeding opportunities they bring into the club. Of course, I wouldn't care about their species, either, if I'd spent the majority of my life being hunted by them."

"Yeah, but we don't live like that anymore. Times are changing."

"Not enough." Andrew wrung out the mop over the sink and rinsed it out with clean water. "Forget about her, Kohl. She's not for you. Her notoriety alone would bring way too much attention to you. To us."

"I know." And he did know. He would never do anything that would bring a threat to their doorstep. Of any kind. Besides, a woman like Devon would never accept someone—some*thing*—like him. Not of her own free will. "I know," he repeated. Whether for Andrew's sake or his own was hard to say.

"Come on, let's go get some sleep. The cleaning crew will take care of the rest of this." Andrew squeezed his shoulder. "There's nothing we can do right now, even if we wanted to. The sun is about to rise."

Actually, it wouldn't be up for a few hours yet. Plenty of time if he knew where Devon lived. Kohl rolled the idea around in his head. He could call the cab company. Or just go to the cab company. Find out who the driver was. Force him to tell him where she lives. He couldn't do the mind-fuck thing, but he could use the scary vampire tactic. Of course, then he'd have to kill the guy or risk exposure. Not something he'd prefer to do, but sometimes it was necessary.

"Kohl."

His thoughts scattered, and he lifted his head to find Andrew waiting for him. "I'm coming." His friend was right. There was nothing to do for it now.

They told Hawke they were heading in, and then made their way to the back door. Not the one by the bathrooms that led outside, but the one at the end of the hallway on the other side of the bar.

Andrew unlocked the combination lock and placed his palm on the sensor pad. There was a soft click, and he pulled the door open, holding it for Kohl. A steel ramp stretched out before them, winding its way to and fro on a gradual decline. At the bottom, they entered another hallway of sorts. Only this one was carved from natural limestone, the same color as the sand that passed for dirt in central Texas.

Soft lighting installed by the coven lit their way. It was needed this far underground where there was no luminosity at all. Even vampires couldn't see in complete and utter darkness, but it was the safest place for their kind, especially during the long central Texas summer.

Kohl's pulse kicked up at the conceived threat of sunlight, guaranteed to burn someone like him to ash within sixty seconds or less, even as the beast within him stretched languidly, longing to bathe its scaly skin in its warmth. It was a continuous tug of war between his two natures he lived with on a daily basis. More than once he'd caught himself heading out the door in the middle of the day, aching to feel the sunshine soaking into his skin, only to make a fast retreat the moment the rays actually touched him.

Down in the caverns, the passage walls were rough to the touch and dripping with moisture from the humidity, and the ceiling was so low in places Kohl had to duck so he didn't bump his head. About fifty feet in, the tunnel widened into a small, natural cavern. The path they were on hugged the wall, and to his left, he looked down over a reservoir filled with a few feet of emerald green water. In the summer, when the rain stopped, it would dry up until it was barely a few inches deep. If it was a bad year of drought, it dried up completely. But vampires didn't need water, other than to bathe, so it made no difference to them. And they had a system rigged that tapped into the city's water for that.

Columns of limestone cluttered the open space, formed from water dripping slowly along the stone over millions of years. He passed by one of the largest stalactites in their home, running his fingertips over the smooth, cool surface as he passed. It had the appearance of hot candle wax melting from the ceiling, and was as big around as a telephone pole—the perfect sentry to stand guard over a forest of smaller stalagmites and stalactites huddled together on the opposite side of the water. A mound of stone pockmarked with crevices in the shapes of tiny doors decorating the front formed the base. He thought of it as the fairy house. Every time he passed it, Kohl half expected to see tiny, magical fairies come fluttering out like butterflies, leaving trails of sparkling fairy dust in their wake.

Though not the first place one would expect vampires to live with all of the technology of the twentieth century, the caverns actually worked out well for them. The temperature was a consistent seventy degrees, and just humid enough. More importantly, this particular series of caves was as yet undiscovered by humans. And the only way to access them was through the building above. Water and electricity was brought down to them from above ground. Cameras strategically mounted in and around the club would alert them to any trespassers who posed a threat, and that threat would be taken out immediately. In a worst-case scenario, the club and the passageway just on the other side of the door would self-destruct. If that happened, it would be up to Kohl to get them all out of the mass grave the coven would then find themselves in. And hopefully, he wouldn't kill anyone in the process.

They followed the path about a quarter mile, through a myriad of passageways and caverns, until it opened up into a room nearly the size of a football field. The ceiling soared over a hundred feet above their heads, featuring a perfectly smooth circle etched into the greater part of the ceiling, the result of a long-gone colony of bats wearing away at the limestone every day as they hid from the sun. Much like the vampires.

And affixed directly in the middle of the cavern, was The Throne.

Like the entirety of the caves, it had been formed naturally from an underground stream that had once moved through the stone, forging it into the shape of a large throne-like structure, with armrests and everything. Above it, a curtain of stalactites hung over the chair, melted together to form a curtain-like formation. Below it, the stone formed natural steps.

In his darkest fantasies, Kohl imagined all of that stone crumbling down onto the head of the male who now sat there. But the Master didn't really deserve that. He wasn't a kind male, or real easy-going. He was an ancient vampire, and set in his ways. But, most of the time, he was fair. He'd also agreed to take in Kohl when he'd had nowhere else to go, even though he was a complete stranger to their coven. Not wholly vampire, but something...other. And for that, he would be forever grateful. It was hard to survive in this world without a group. The saying was true, there was safety in numbers.

The coven leader turned his head as he and Andrew walked in, his long, blond hair hanging to his waist. It was often spotted with dried blood from his last meal, giving him the look of a hyena. His form was solid and stocky, without a soft spot on him. Huge forearms used to wielding battle-axes rested on the cold stone, and thighs as big around as tree trunks tested the endurance of his worn leather pants.

Dark eyes narrowed on the two of them, and the Master held up a palm the size of a grizzly's, quieting the others in the room. Some of them had been up in the club when the shooting happened, some had not.

Kohl spotted Jaz at the edge of the crowd, easy to pick out with his long, black hair and telltale jean vest he'd been "gifted" from a biker in California. The vampire grinned, his broken fang in full view, and toasted Kohl with his cup. Probably filled with the blood of one of the shooting victims. After a measuring glance, Kohl gave him a nod and looked away. Though Jaz never spoke of how he'd lost his fang, Kohl knew it had to have been a traumatic experience, even for a vampire. He knew this because Jaz's state of mind was what was referred to in the vampire community as "fragile," and he was often given some slack for his actions where others were not. But, they were family, and they all watched his back, and kept him from getting into any serious trouble.

"Kohl. Come here, please." Voices fell to hushed whispers as the Master's deep timbre echoed through the cavern.

Andrew slapped him on the shoulder, and with a small bow to the Master, wandered off to his room—one of the smaller caverns down a passageway behind The Throne. No one went anywhere without passing within sight or hearing of the Master. He kept a close eye on his coven. Kohl couldn't blame him. It was mostly made up of a group of misfit vampires who, for one reason or another, had had to leave their original families.

He walked up to the Master, and went down on one knee. An old-school way to show respect, but one that was still insisted upon. "Master." He realized at that moment he didn't even know the vampire's born name.

"Get up. And tell me what happened upstairs."

He did as ordered, a tingle of apprehension lifting the hair on the back of his neck. "You haven't gotten the full report, yet?"

"I saw the shooters on the cameras. I also saw you move faster than any bullet to dive across the dance floor to save a woman. A *human* woman." The word was spit out of his mouth like a mouthful of moldy broccoli.

Kohl rubbed the slight ache in his hip unconsciously. He'd nearly forgotten getting hit. There was a tear in his pants, one in front and one in back, where the bullet had gone through, and the material was stiff with dried blood. The wound had healed quickly. Still... "I wouldn't say I was faster."

The Master dropped his eyes to the tear and huffed, something between a laugh and a reprimand. "Stop fucking around, and explain to me why you put us all in jeopardy."

"I honestly don't know." Kohl scratched the back of his neck before shoving his hands in his front pockets. "I didn't think about it. I just did it." He paused. "I fucked up," he added.

"You'd better believe you fucked up. I don't like leaving witnesses, Kohl."

That now familiar heat scalded the back of Kohl's neck. "She doesn't remember what happened. Andrew made sure of it." He fought and failed to keep a level tone as the beast raised its head, and he wondered how far he would go to protect this woman.

Pretty damn far, he decided, if the fact that he was about to breathe fire on the coven Master was any indication.

His leader cocked his head, then leaned forward in his chair, his leather pants creaking in protest. "Kohl—"

"I know. I can't see her again."

The Master's eyes flashed, and Kohl checked himself, removing the bite from his tone, but unable to do anything about the unhappiness of the beast within. "I know. I won't do anything to risk exposing the club. Or us." Even as he attempted to defuse the situation, his gums itched and then burned as his fangs broke through the surface. His skin tingled, the hair on his body standing straight up as heat zig-zagged across the surface.

After a moment, the Master sighed, a great heaving of his massive chest, and the beast settled back down again. "Good. You know I don't like being a hardass—"

Kohl bit down on both lips to keep from laughing out loud.

"But this isn't something I'm willing to give way on. Humans cannot find out about us."

Crossing his arms over his chest, Kohl begged to differ. "Some already know about us, and they haven't caused us any harm. And she happens to be one of them. Actually, she's known about us for years. She doesn't pose a threat." He could've bitten his own tongue off the moment the words were out of his mouth.

The Master became very still. "What do you mean 'she knows about us'? I thought you told me Andrew wiped her memory?"

There was no way out now but to tell the truth. "He did. The ones of last night, and me."

"Then how does she know of us?"

Dammit. Why the fuck did he open his mouth? "Andrew wiped her memory of the shooting, but she already knew about our kind before she came here. She used to work for Parasupe, Inc."

The Master sat back in his throne. Kohl watched as the blood rose in his cheeks until his face was a deep, ruddy, red. Their leader didn't like being caught unaware, but there'd be less of a chance of that if the old vampire would embrace modern technology.

They all knew the company. Parasupe—a ridiculously obvious combination of "paranormal" and "supernatural"—

posed as some sort of environmental protection company. It was the activists who had made Devon's life hell. But what the company really did was keep an eye on all of the vampires, shifters, and other supernatural creatures who resided in the fine state of Texas. And they were quickly expanding across the country.

The thing was, though, the humans who ran the company didn't know the supernatural community was aware of them. However, when your friends with fangs started disappearing with no explanation, you damn well better believe it won't take long for others of their kind to find out who was removing them from the equation.

"You said she *used* to work there. She no longer does?"

"No. Something happened a while back. I don't know all the details, no one does except the humans who were in the courtroom when it all went down, but I think she was a whistleblower of some sort or another."

"What is that, exactly?"

"A whistleblower is someone who sees something wrong happening within the company they work for. Something serious enough to report. Something that could potentially get another person fired or the company shut down."

"So, she did this to them?"

"Yes."

"And she is still alive?"

"Thanks to what I did tonight, yes."

Kohl was glad to see the color recede as the Master rubbed his jaw with one hand. He really didn't want to deal with one of his temper tantrums right now. But his next words were not something he ever would've expected.

"I want you to find out what happened between her and her

company." He nodded to himself. "Yes, find her. She will trust you instinctively, even if she doesn't remember you or what you did. You played the hero tonight. Her blood will recognize you."

Her blood will recognize you. Kohl inhaled sharply, a rush of exhilaration making him lightheaded. The beast, sensing his excitement, stirred, and he silently cursed the reminder of why he could never act on these feelings.

"Kohl."

His name brought him back to the present. "Yeah?"

"Find her. Tonight."

The beast stretched its wings as Kohl clenched his jaw and nodded.

CHAPTER 4

CURRENT DAY

The Caves looked different in the daylight, more like an old trading post than an exclusive nightclub. But Devon knew firsthand that looks could be deceiving, and its innocent appearance was part of its disguise. It blended in with the rest of the ramshackle buildings interspersed throughout the area, and didn't call attention to itself.

She got out of the car and locked her purse inside, shoving the keys in the front pocket of her hoodie. The wind whipped her hair around her face, along with a few stray raindrops, but it looked like the weather would continue to hold.

The entry was locked, so she walked the perimeter of the building until she found the back door, her sneakers crunching on the gravel. Looking around, she saw a camera perched high up in the corner of the eaves, and another in a scraggly tree behind her, facing the door. She was certain there must be more she would never find, probably hidden within the groups of prickly pear cactus and wired into the telephone poles.

Or, maybe not. Maybe they just had ordinary cameras.

She studied the barren landscape, even more so now that it was winter. The tree with the broken branch, that cluster of cactus—it all felt way too familiar to her, and she wracked her brain as to why. But the only thing she managed to resurrect was her headache. Besides, she would've had no reason to be back here.

Convinced she was imagining things in her efforts to remember, she tried the door, and to her surprise, it was unlocked.

Devon paused before she walked in. She had no idea why she was there, or what she'd expected to find inside. But something had drawn her back to this place, and she always trusted her instincts, even if it cost her—her job, her reputation, her relationship, her life.

Yeah, it didn't always work out easily or the way she would've hoped. But at least she could live with herself, even if it *was* still in Texas. The last place she'd ever thought she'd live. It was too hot, and too cold. And too...Texas. Though Austin actually wasn't that bad. She liked it a lot more than Dallas.

A calm determination filled her as she stared at her hand on the knob, and she yanked the door open. She wasn't worried about the cameras. It wasn't like she was breaking in. The door was left unlocked. If they didn't want just anyone walking in there, then they needed to take better precautions.

She also wasn't worried about anyone being there. Well, at least she didn't think anyone would be there. Not unless the vampires employed humans to clean up during the day while they slept. And if that was the case, she'd just tell whoever was working that she'd lost her cell phone, which was inside her purse back in the car, so her story would sound legit.

Mind made up, she went inside, letting the door bang shut loudly behind her. "Hello?" The familiar smells of booze, sweaty bodies, and the acrid stench from the smoke machines stroked her memory a little more.

Something had happened here last night. She was sure of it. And she had the creepiest feeling that it hadn't been sweaty dancing and sweatier sex in the bathroom.

"Hello?" she called out again, but no one responded or came running to see who the hell had walked in their back door. Devon wandered down the hall, passing the bathrooms and a door that actually *was* locked—the office, maybe—and came out just to the right of the bar. The dance floor spread out before her, lit only by a single light above the bar.

Devon studied that light, and the bar area beneath it. She remembered the bartenders. Both muscled and tatted up. Both brunette. One short with spiky hair, and maybe Korean. But the other guy—the tall one with the dark hair and the short beard who'd made her drink—he'd been watching her the entire night. Staring, really. And with such intensity that it still made her skin tingle just thinking about it.

Devon had actually kind of hoped it was because of an actual interest in her, and not because of her notorious past. Parasupe thought the supernatural creatures they monitored weren't aware of their activities. But Devon knew that was all a bunch of bullshit. They had to be aware. They weren't stupid. And most of them, the vampires especially, had a keen intelligence and charisma about them that was near irresistible. It practically oozed from this new vampire. It was why she'd pushed her way up to his side of the bar, even though the other side had been less crowded. Sex was something she hadn't had in so long, she didn't even care if it was that good. However, she would bet good money that the big guy behind the bar would be fucking *awesome* at sex. Real, raw, dirty, earthy sex. Because there wasn't one thing about him that didn't scream sexy dominance, simmering beneath the surface. And she would've given just about anything to have that boil over onto her.

But she'd been wrong. He hadn't been interested in her as a woman. He'd just felt sorry for her. Which, sadly, she had to admit was a better reaction than she normally got. A wave of melancholy and missed opportunities washed over her, and she turned away from the bar.

To her left, across the open dance floor, chairs were stacked on top of shiny round tables, and another light was on in the far corner. The lingering scent of bleach hit her nose, and she was impressed with the cleanliness of the place. Of course, it wouldn't last long. People were horribly inconsiderate about the messes they made in places like this, especially when they were drinking.

Walking around the bar, she saw another hallway leading toward the back. "Hello?" she called as she headed down it. Oddly enough, there were no offices or bathrooms, just an empty hallway leading to a door. Which was strange, because she was positive there was only one back door that led outside —the one she'd just come in.

As she approached, she noticed a pad off to the side. One that looked like it read finger or palm prints. A deadlock bolted the door above the latch.

Something was down there. Something the vampires definitely didn't want anyone to find. Their den, perhaps?

Knowing there was no way she was getting in there, and not really convinced she wanted to go through that door even if she could, Devon turned to leave. She didn't know what the hell had made her come here, but she obviously wasn't getting any answers today. The place was spotless and empty. No one was around. Maybe she could come back tonight, though. Now that she'd been inside once, she hoped it wouldn't be a problem to get in again.

She heard the latch click right before the door opened behind her.

Devon spun around to find the bartender from last night. The hot one. The one who'd been watching her. She froze, surprised to see him awake in the middle of the day, and unsure of what to say.

He gave her his back, closing the door behind him and resetting the combination lock before he turned around. "We're closed," he said, not unkindly.

His voice was deep, had the barest hint of a country drawl, and a sexy bite of gravel. Devon found it extremely sensual, like he'd just woken up, and she wondered if that was the case or if he always sounded that way when he wasn't shouting over the music. Dark hair, the same soft black as his close-cut beard, was cut short and pushed back from his face except for a few stray pieces that fell over his forehead. Sweet brown eyes stared down at her, lingering on her chest a moment too long before they moved back up to her face. Devon was tall for a woman, so he had to be at least six-foot-two or -three. A black T-shirt and worn jeans hugged his muscular frame. Tattoos covered the sides of his neck, the length of his arms, and even his hands.

Her face flamed when he smiled with a slight lift to his eyebrows. "Can I help you with something?"

Devon pushed her hood off her head and attempted to smooth her hair, tucking in stray pieces that had escaped her ponytail. "Um, my phone." Closing her eyes, she shook her head as she gave an awkward laugh. When she opened them again, he was studying her, a slight tilt to his head, the corners of his mouth still curved slightly upward, like he wasn't sure if he should laugh with her or call the men with the little white coats.

She took a breath. "I was here last night, I don't know if you remember."

"I remember."

"Oh." His admission threw her off for a few seconds. She took a breath and continued. "I lost my cell phone. I think maybe I lost it here…somewhere." She stuck out her hand. "I'm Devon, by the way. Devon Young."

His eyes dropped to her hand, and for a moment, she didn't think he was going to take it.

Just when she was about to pull her hand back, he reached out and closed his fingers around hers with a firm grip. "I'm Kohl. With a 'K'. Uh, K-O-H-L. Kohl Sergones."

The heat radiating off his skin surprised her. Never having actually touched a vampire before, she'd always thought they would be cold. But she recovered quickly and returned his handshake. Her hand felt tiny and fragile in his grip, and she knew he would only have to exert the smallest amount of pressure to break the bones. "Let me guess. Sergones, with an 'S'."

He dropped his eyes with an embarrassed twist of his mouth, an intriguing show of vulnerability she wasn't expecting from a guy like him. Vampire or not.

She smiled, and tried to put him at ease. "Hi, Kohl. It's nice to meet you."

His eyes shot up, travelling over her features as though he were attempting to memorize her face. Then his large shoulders relaxed and he returned her smile with a timid one of his own as he gave her hand a small squeeze and released it. "I tend to talk too much when I'm nervous," he admitted.

"Are you nervous?"

Shoving his hands in his front pockets, he turned on the charm she remembered from the night before. "Only around pretty ladies." He grinned.

The air rushed from her lungs. Not from the compliment. From that smile. He was beautiful when his entire face lit up like that.

"Thank you," she managed.

He rubbed the back of his neck, the muscles in his arm flexing, and he suddenly looked as if he'd rather be anywhere else. "I'm pretty positive your cell isn't here. The club is checked every night after we close before the cleaning crew comes in, and if anything is found, it's brought to the bar and put inside the safe. No one brought anything to me or Andrew that I can recall. But I can check for you and make sure."

"That's not really necessary—" Maybe she'd misread his intentions. Maybe he smiled like that at everyone and was used to sweet-talking women. He was a bartender, after all. Flirting was how he made his tips.

But he was already walking around her.

Devon watched him pass. He moved with an easy grace she could only hope to achieve someday—and probably never would—his strides long and smooth. Yet, the ease of movement didn't quite succeed in covering the raw power she sensed was carefully restrained. She imagined he always had to be aware not to appear "other." Vampires were capable of many inhuman traits—speed, mind control, and superior strength, just to name those that were well-known by people like her.

Eyes on his broad back, she followed him back down the hallway. When she got to the bar, he was already behind it, opening the small safe beneath the register. Guilt plagued her for lying to him. "Um, really, you don't have to do this. I'll take your word for it. I probably just dropped it in my car or something."

He gave her a quick glance and opened the door of the safe, then backed away and indicated for her to look for herself.

Feeling rather foolish, she walked over and bent down to peer inside. It was completely empty. "Yeah. It's not in there. But, thanks for letting me look for myself." She straightened and took a quick step back so he could lock it up again...

And hit a wall of pure, hard muscle as he stepped forward at the same time.

His arm snaked around her, trapping her arms to her sides and holding her tight against him. Warm breath teased the curls that had escaped her ponytail, tickling her cheek. Curling his big body around her, he breathed in the scent of her hair before slowly moving down to her throat.

Devon froze, her heart racing in her chest even as her breath arrested in her lungs. Tingles of fear and arousal chased each other across her skin.

His voice rumbled just behind her right ear. "I won't hurt you, Devon." Something between a growl of restraint and a purr of pleasure followed his words.

The hair on the back of her neck stood up and a chill shivered down her spine. But she held completely still, wondering every moment if this would be her last. She was stupid. Lured by the charisma and the sweet smile, she'd forgotten for a moment who—or rather, *what*—she was dealing with.

And yet, beneath the panic, ripples of desire heated her blood and tightened the muscles low in her stomach. She felt every inch of him against her. Every tiny shift of muscle. Every breath. Every heartbeat.

He nuzzled her neck, still making that noise, and without conscious thought, she tilted her head away to make more room for him even as her mind screamed at her to get away. She gave herself a hard internal shake. "Kohl? What are you doing?"

"You smell so good," he told her. "Come to dinner with me tonight, Devon."

Something scraped her skin. A fang? But the sting was there and gone so fast she wasn't completely sure she hadn't imagined it, replaced by a brush of his lips so soft it made her shudder. "Am I the main course?" The second the words were out of her mouth, she wished she could take them back.

He chuckled, deep and low. "No. At least, not tonight. I like to get to know my victims a little before I feed on them."

Devon frowned. Was he teasing her? "Then why are you holding me here like this?"

"You touched me and…I didn't think." He inhaled deeply, pulling her in tighter. "I'm sorry. I don't want to scare you."

He was hard. She could feel him against her. "You're holding me against my will, Kohl." Actually, what he was doing was pretty much the most exciting thing that had happened to her in a long time. But it was also the most dangerous. She needed to remember that. "You're scaring me a little."

As soon as the words were out of her mouth, he stilled

against her. His arm immediately disappeared and the warmth of his body left her back.

She shivered again, this time from the cold.

"I'm sorry. That wasn't my intention, Devon." His voice was raw.

She turned around, drawn by the distress in his tone, but he took a step back and lowered his chin, staring hard at the floor between them so she couldn't see his face. One arm crossed his body, his hand resting on the opposite shoulder.

Her eyes narrowed at the familiarity of the gesture. He was hiding. That's why he'd pulled her up against him. So she wouldn't see who he was. "I know what you are, Kohl. You don't have to worry about that. You don't have to hide."

Eyes lit from within flashed up to her face, more fiery gold than brown now. He studied her for a few seconds, then dropped his arm. "I'm sorry I scared you," he repeated, and she could see the tips of his fangs peeking out from beneath his upper lip. "I just...reacted, and then I panicked. And then I reacted to the panic. I forgot you were familiar with—" He made a circle with his finger, encompassing his face. "This."

He was wrong. Though she knew they existed, and had read a lot about them from the reports that came in, she wasn't used to seeing vampires up close and personal. It wasn't part of her job description. She'd been more behind the scenes than in the field. Devon took the chance to study him, enticed by the way he ran the tip of his tongue over his exposed fangs, and for the briefest of instances, she wondered what it would feel like to be bit.

He sighed heavily, and looked off to the side, breaking the connection. Then he frowned, and when he turned back, his eyes were back to their normal brown. "Does this mean you won't go to dinner with me?"

Devon laughed. She couldn't help it. This entire conversation was ridiculous. "That all depends."

One eyebrow lifted in silent question. "On?"

Her fear of him overridden by the raw lust still heating her blood, she said the first thing that came to her mind. "On whether or not you're going to expect sex as a thank you."

He stilled again. It was eerie the way he could do that. There wasn't the slightest movement in his large body that she could see. Then he leaned in toward her. "Is there room to negotiate?"

A smile spread across her face. "There's always room to negotiate, but no guarantees on the outcome."

Kohl gave her a nod, seemingly satisfied with her answer. "I'll pick you up just after dark."

"I'll be ready."

Their eyes caught and held, and they grinned at each other until Kohl broke it off, glancing toward the hall. "I would walk you to your car, but, you know, I burn easily. Even on cloudy days such as this."

"It's okay. I can see myself out." She turned to go, but he took her arm, staying her. Tingles ran all the way up to her shoulder. "What?" she asked.

Those warm brown eyes travelled over her face. "I do remember you, Devon. And I'm very glad you came back here today."

His declaration, if that's what it was, took her by surprise. She didn't know what to say, so she said nothing.

"You're parked out front?"

She nodded.

"I'll let you out."

He came toward her, placing his hand on the small of her back. His palm was warm, even through her hoodie. Devon allowed him to steer her in the right direction, a sense of déjà vu teasing the edges of her memory.

Did he touch her like this last night? Why didn't she remember?

At the door, he pulled the keys from his pocket and unlocked the door. He stayed out of the reach of the light as he opened it for her. "I'll see you tonight."

"Okay."

She heard the lock click as he shut it behind her.

Devon walked back to her car in a daze. Had she just agreed to have dinner with a vampire? Was she really that hard up?

But as she started the engine and made her way back out to the highway, she knew it had nothing to do with desperation, and everything to do with Kohl.

CHAPTER 5

Kohl wasn't able to sleep the remainder of the day, not that he ever slept much anyway.

He'd thought he was hallucinating when he saw Devon on his computer monitor. Thought it had only been wishful thinking that the person lurking around outside, face concealed by the hood of their pullover sweatshirt, was actually her. But then she'd looked up, directly at the camera in the trees behind her, before she'd turned and yanked open the door someone had foolishly left unlocked in all of the commotion the night before, and he'd nearly knocked his chair over in his rush to get to her before someone else noticed she was inside the club.

Luckily, Kohl had been the only one monitoring the cameras, and his living space in the caverns wasn't near the others, so no one saw him run out. For safety reasons, his room was on the opposite side of the throne room than everyone else's, deep within a cave on the far side of the underground aquifer. The space was large enough for the beast to spread its wings if it happened to get out, but too small for it to escape without making enough noise to warn the others. Not by their choice, but by his. He never wanted to take the chance of someone he cared about being too close and getting hurt. Or worse.

So no one saw him jog up the ramp that would take him aboveground, and no one saw him come back down thirty minutes later and go back to his rooms. He would tell the Master what he'd learned from Devon after their dinner tonight, but he wasn't telling anyone of their plans beforehand. It may be overcautious of him, but he didn't want to take the chance of being followed. He loved his coven, but he didn't trust them. At least, not all of them. Most would do what the Master bade without question. However, some did whatever the fuck they wanted without a care for the consequences, and somehow always got away with it.

As he got ready for his dinner date with Devon, his mind was spinning and his hands were shaking. And one had nothing to do with the other.

Hawke poked his head inside the room as Kohl was getting dressed. "Hey. You want to go to the city with us tonight?"

Kohl finished fastening the buttons on his blue dress shirt and ran his fingers through his damp hair. It was all he ever did after he washed it. "I can't. Maybe next time."

"That's what you always say." Leaning back against the wall, Hawke crossed his arms and ankles and stared at him intently. "You know I wouldn't let anything happen, right? I wouldn't let you hurt anybody."

Kohl glanced over at his friend, silently debating whether he should tuck his shirt into his dark gray slacks. They had this conversation at least once a week. "There's nothing you would be able to do if the beast appeared, Hawke." Looking in the mirror above his dresser, he decided to leave it out.

"I wish you would stop calling it that. You're not a 'beast'. You have the blood of the dreki." Rolling the "r", he pronounced the word in perfect Icelandic, the home of Kohl's mother's people. "The blood of a proud thunder of dragons. Even the Master knows your worth. It's why he took you in. You're like his own personal guard dog...or guard dragon. I don't know why you're so ashamed of it."

"I'm not ashamed. But that's not why he took me in. The only reason he allows me to stay here is—"

"Because you are also a vampire. You're one of us. You have been since your mother brought you here."

"I'm half dreki." He slipped his shoes on. He was tired of arguing about it.

"Half dragon. And half vampire." Hawke pushed away from the wall and came to stand near him, picking up the book on his dresser and glancing at the cover without any real interest. "Don't you realize how rare that is? How rare *you* are?"

Kohl met his passionate gaze. "Yeah. I do. And so does the Master. And that's why he keeps me around. He collects oddities. Just like it's the only reason he keeps that bastard Jaz around with his one fang."

Hawke snorted, putting the book back where it was. "That's *not* why he keeps you around."

"Okay, it's because I'm the best chance you all have of surviving if the coven is discovered by anyone who'd want to hurt us. The beast is the only one who'd be able to break us out."

"I can't argue with that. You *are* our best shot." He grinned and slapped Kohl on the shoulder. "And hopefully, you won't burn us all to ash while you're busting us out. As to Jaz…" He shrugged. "I, for one, wouldn't be heartbroken if he decided to move on to another coven. Or to hell. Whichever. I'm tired of watching his ass all the time. I'm not a fucking babysitter."

"I hear ya."

Hawke stepped back and eyed Kohl up and down, as if noticing what he was wearing for the first time. "What's with the fancy outfit if you're not going out with us? You're not working tonight."

Kohl turned away from the sharp eyes of his friend, and checked out his appearance in the mirror again, smoothing invisible wrinkles. His shirt was tailored to fit him, as were the slacks. He was too large to buy stuff off the rack. No tie tonight, and he'd left the top three buttons open. His tattoo of purple roses—his mother's favorite flower—peeked out from the open neckline.

Hawke met his eyes in the mirror with an expectant look on his face.

Knowing he wasn't getting out of there without answering, Kohl debated making up some bullshit story. But in the end, he told the truth. Hawke was like a brother to him, and the only one he trusted implicitly. Plus, he wanted someone to know where he was going and with who. Just in case. "Remember the woman from last night?"

"Devon. The girl from the news."

"Yeah."

Hawke dropped his head back in disbelief. "Kohl, we discussed this. She's cute, yeah, and I'm sure she's smart and funny and probably a hellion in bed, but she's way too high profile."

Kohl bared his fangs at the bed comment. Just a little.

Hawke raised his eyebrows as if to say, *really?*

"Sorry," Kohl muttered. "I know. And I swear, I wasn't going to go anywhere near her. But the Master ordered it. He wants to know what she knows about us. Didn't he tell you?"

Hawke looked confused. "So, he knows you're seeing her tonight."

"No."

"But, you just said—"

"I said he wants me to find out about her. That doesn't mean I trust him."

"Yeah, well, can't say I blame you there." His brow furrowed in thought. "I wonder why he wants you to see her..."

"I told you. He wants to know what she knows. There must be something, or she wouldn't have Parasupe trying to gun her down in the middle of a club." Kohl's stomach twisted at the thought of betraying her to the Master, but he didn't see that he had a choice. Not unless he could think of a way out of it.

That caught Hawke's attention. "Didn't you hear? The shooters weren't from Parasupe."

Kohl paused with his wallet halfway in his pocket. "What? Who were they, then?"

"We don't know. But one of them took a minute to die last night, and apparently he told Mark he'd been compelled to do it. He died before he could give up a name."

"So, they were just there to shoot up our club?"

Hawke shook his head. "They were there for Devon. That much I was right about."

The back of his neck burned, and Kohl rubbed it unconsciously as he began to pace. "He just offered up this information?"

Hawke snorted. "Hell, no. Mark used compulsion." He

studied Kohl closely. "What are you going to do about Devon?"

Kohl stopped in front of him. "I'm gonna play along. For now. I'll tell the Master what I find out. Later."

"When no one can follow you and hurt her."

"Exactly."

"I gotcha." Hawke wandered over to the tunnel that would take him out of Kohl's area and back out to the throne room. He paused before he left. "You're not taking her anywhere populated, right? And you know to call me if anything happens with…." He waved his hand up and down Kohl's body.

Kohl checked his back pockets to make sure he'd remembered his wallet and phone. "No. And yes."

"Good." Hawke turned to leave, but paused a second time. "I think."

Kohl grinned. "She did say we could negotiate the price of dinner."

Shaking his head, Hawke laughed as he led the way out.

Kohl arrived at Devon's apartments thirty minutes after the sun dipped below the horizon. He walked up the stairs, completely aware of his surroundings. Despite his precautions, he looked around one last time to check he wasn't followed before entering the building. Halfway down the interior hallway, he found her apartment and knocked.

Something crashed to the floor on the other side of the door, followed by a string of soft curses that was quite impressive in its creativity, and then she was there, standing in the open doorway with a small, round basket filled with keys and notepads in her hand.

And suddenly he couldn't breathe.

Her dark hair was down in a full mass of soft curls that fell around her face in sexy disorder. She wore little makeup that he could tell, just an outline around her eyes and some color on her plump lips.

He wanted to kiss those lips. The urge to taste them came upon him so strong and sudden he even leaned toward her a little before he remembered himself and snapped up straight. But he couldn't stop his eyes from traveling down her body. Tonight, she wore flat-heeled black shoes, a pair of dark jeans that hugged her hips and thighs, and a silky looking red top—the exact color of blood when it first left the body—open at the throat just enough to expose a "V" of smooth skin. She had a small beauty mark that was slightly off center at the bottom of her throat. A solitary diamond pendant sparkled just above the swell of her breasts, slightly larger than the one in her nose.

Her eyes widened as she took in his appearance. "I think I'm underdressed. Let me go change. I'll just be a minute." She set the basket down on a side table that sat near the door and started walking away before he could answer, leaving him on the other side of the threshold. "Uh, Devon—"

She stopped and turned. "Oh! I'm sorry. Please, Kohl. Come in."

He did, shutting the door behind him. "You don't need to change. You look...stunning."

"But you're all dressed up and I just threw on some jeans."

"I like your jeans," he told her honestly. "I *really* like your jeans."

She stared at him wide-eyed a moment, then burst out laughing, and he felt himself relax as he grinned back at her without shame.

When she could speak again, she put her hands on her hips.

The movement widened the "V" at her throat, exposing more of her sun-kissed brown skin. "Well, where are we going? And I'll decide if I need to put on something nicer."

Kohl tore his eyes away from her neckline, his tongue touching the tips of his fangs before he spoke, attempting to ease the ache there before they fully descended and made him look like some kind of prepubescent vampire who had no self control. "Actually, I thought we could have a picnic. Somewhere away from the crowds, if that's okay? It's a warm night for January, but I don't think it's going to rain. I have a blanket, and I can start a fire. I also picked up some food for you on the way over. I wasn't sure what you liked, so I just got a little of everything. And wine. White and red. I don't know what you prefer…"

He trailed off as she stared at him with a smile touching her lips, her head tilted to the side. "I'm talking too much again." Shoving his hands in his pockets to hide his nervousness, he looked down at his shoes, wondering what the hell was the matter with him.

Something about this woman just…undid him.

"A picnic would be nice. Honestly, I really don't like going out in public much, for obvious reasons. Let me grab my coat."

He exhaled the breath he'd been holding as she walked into another room. Without her taking up his focus, he noticed his surroundings for the first time. The apartment was roughly the size of a shoebox. He could reach the opposite wall in three strides. And he knew that because he counted as he walked over to the window.

But the view of downtown Austin was beautiful. The city lights sparkled against the night sky like something out of a movie. He glanced up, hoping the weather would hold. It was cloudy, which was good because it wasn't too cold for her. But it also meant things could change at any moment. Texas weather was unpredictable as fuck.

"Okay, I'm ready." Her black jacket fell just below her hips and looked warm.

After making sure she locked her door behind them, he escorted her out of the building to his ride.

When she saw it, parked in the guest spot directly in front of the building, she pulled up short. "Wow. I'm glad I didn't change into a dress."

Kohl studied her reaction, wishing he had Hawke's gift of reading people. "We can take your car if you'd be more comfortable."

A huge grin broke out across her face, lighting up the night, and he lost his breath once more.

"Oh, hell no. This is perfect." She grabbed his wrist and pulled him forward. "Come on, Kohl!" Without waiting for him, she threw a leg over the seat of his Harley and put her hands on the grips as she admired the matte black paint job.

He had to admit, she looked damn fine straddling all that power.

"How do you start this monster?"

"It's a 2014 Harley Fatboy." Kohl unbuckled the helmet from the strap of the saddlebag and handed it to her. "And we're not going anywhere until you put this on."

Rolling her eyes, she took the helmet from him and stuck it on her head. "What about you?"

"I'll be all right."

All of the light left her face and she was suddenly serious. "Oh. That's right. I almost forgot for a minute."

He watched her intently. "Does it bother you that much?

That I'm not like you?"

Devon met his eyes as she buckled the strap under her chin. "No. Not tonight."

"Are you sure?"

The smile returned, not as bright as it was, but still there. "I'm sure."

But the shift in her energy didn't match her words, and Kohl felt a sharp prick of pain in the center of his chest. It swiftly stretched and grew until his sternum felt on the verge of collapse, and he silently cursed. Vampire emotions ran higher than humans, but dragons...well, dragons were jacked up empaths. Between the two, Kohl felt things on a level that was unheard of, even for other supernatural creatures. "Devon. I won't hurt you."

She frowned, her hands falling into her lap. "I know you won't."

She sounded more convinced than he felt. "Good." He approached the bike and indicated for her to scoot back.

With a sigh of disappointment, she did.

Kohl lifted the bike off the kickstand and got on in front of her, glad he'd worn pants with a little give. He made sure it was in neutral, put the key in the switch on top of the gas tank, turned it to the on position, and pushed the start button.

The engine rumbled to life as Devon's arms slid around his waist. She linked her fingers at the waistline of his pants and leaned into him, her open coat falling to either side of his hips. He was so aware of her, he could feel the heat of her skin and the lace of her bra through her shirt. His cock, semi-hard since she'd opened the door to her apartment, swelled to an uncomfortable size. Kohl had never been so grateful that he had no need for protection against the cold.

He kicked the bike into gear and eased out into downtown traffic, needing to focus on something other than his passenger. He managed, barely, even with her full breasts pressed against his back and his ass nestled between her thighs.

The forty-minute ride was way too short, and he spent most of it wishing they could just keep going. Leave everyone and everything behind and live on the road, with the cool night air in his face and this woman tucked up warm against his back.

But instead, Kohl slowed down and turned onto a narrow paved road, ducking his head to avoid the low hanging branches of the trees that formed a canopy overhead. They'd left the city a while back, and a few minutes later, he saw moonlight glittering on the surface of a large lake as it peeked through the clouds.

The road ended abruptly, dead-ending into the grass, and Kohl turned the bike so it faced back the way they'd just came and turned off the engine. The gentle lapping of water hitting the shoreline and an easy breeze rustling through the trees were the only sounds he heard. It was too early in the year for the hum of cicadas or the songs of crickets. And other than some rabbits and perhaps a coyote or two, most of the animals in the area were sure to be hunkered down for the night.

Putting the kickstand down, he braced the bike while Devon climbed off. She pulled off her helmet, trying to fix her hair as she looked around. "What is this place? It's got to be someone's property. Is it okay that we're here?"

He opened one of the saddlebags and pulled out a blanket and a battery-operated lantern. "It's mine."

She swung around to look at him. "Yours? This land is yours?"

"Yup." He walked out into the grass and found a good spot close to the water. "I bought it a while back, before everyone started moving out here."

"That must have been a long time ago."

He didn't answer, wondering if knowing his true age would bother her.

Eventually Devon looked around again. "How big is your lot?"

"It's about ten acres."

"Ten acres of lakefront property. Wow."

Kohl laid the blanket out and glanced around as he rolled up his sleeves. At one time, he'd had thoughts of building a home here. A place for him and his mom where they could be themselves. Back then, the closest neighbor was miles away. But after she'd died, it took him a long time to come back here. And by that time, humans had started buying up the available land surrounding his property.

"I hired people to keep an acre mowed and free of fire ant mounds, and to take care of the trees—" He glanced overhead and she followed his gaze. Mostly tall, leafy oaks and maples, which is what had attracted him to this acreage in particular, even though he'd never be able to enjoy warm days on the lake. "The rest of the land I'm leaving the way nature intended."

"What are you going to do with it?"

He glanced at Devon as he turned on the lantern and set it beside the blanket. "Nothing."

She followed him back to the bike, reaching into the other saddlebag to help him carry the food he'd brought. "Nothing? You're not gonna build a house? Maybe live here someday?" She paused with a container of strawberries in her hand, her face screwed up in thought. "It would have to have a basement,

I guess. I don't know if they could dig that far into the ground here. It's all limestone." She grabbed the loaf of French bread. "You could have it basement-like on the first floor. No windows. No way for the sun to get in. A sealed entrance. Then have a second floor that's nothing but windows. With a deck that has stairs that lead down to the water. And you could put in a dock..." She wandered off to put her haul of food on the blanket.

A striking image of Devon standing on the deck with a glass of wine in her hand, her curves silhouetted against the setting sun, shot through his head. Or lying in the sun down by the water in nothing but bikini bottoms. He could almost feel the warmth of her skin, and taste the saltiness of the sweat glistening between her breasts. Sorrow filled him that he'd never be able to witness such a beautiful sight.

Kohl cleared his throat as she came back to the bike. "I'm not sure. Maybe. Someday." He took the wine bottles from her and went to the blanket to arrange their picnic.

But she wasn't done yet. "So, you own all of this property, and you're just going to...do nothing with it? Just leave it wild except for this area by the water?"

Shoving his hands in his front pockets, he smiled. "Yeah."

"Why?"

Kohl shrugged. "So no one else can build on it. It's a safe place."

"Safe for whom?"

"For me. For the animals that lived here first."

She eyed him strangely for a moment, and again, he wished he could reach into her head so he'd know what she was thinking. Then she looked down at the food he'd spread out on the blanket. Her stomach growled, and she kneeled down on the edge, brushing off the loose grass before she sat cross-legged and picked up the bag of sliced French bread. She layered soft cheese on top, folded it together, and took a bite. "This is amazing, Kohl," she said between bites. "Thank you. I'm starving."

"Are you cold? I can build a fire."

"I'm good." She patted the blanket beside her.

Kohl sank down beside her, leaning back on his hands and stretching his legs out in front of him.

He watched her mouth as she ate. Watched her eyes close with pleasure at the taste of the food. Her joy with something so simple was palpable. "I'm glad you like it. I wasn't sure what I should bring."

Her hands, each holding a chunk of bread and cheese, fell into her lap as she looked out over the water and sighed. "This is perfect."

She was beautiful sitting there in the glow of the lantern. And when she looked back at him, her eyes exuded a warmth Kohl wasn't sure what to do with. It wasn't like he hadn't been with women before, of course he had. He'd had his share of women all over Texas. Not that they would remember, because he'd always had Hawke wipe their memories when he was finished. But he'd never been this affected by them. Not like he was with Devon.

Needing something to quench the thirst that had suddenly erupted in his soul, he reached for the closest bottle of wine and popped the cork. Tipping it up to his mouth, he took a healthy swig.

Devon was staring at him when he lowered it again.

"What?"

"You can drink wine?"

Puzzled, he just nodded.

"Do you eat?"

He shook his head. "I thought you knew about us. About me."

She grabbed a French fry he'd gotten from the fast food joint down the road from her apartment and took a bite, chewing thoughtfully. "I never worked directly with...people such as yourself."

It was the perfect opening to find out what he needed to know, but he wanted to tread carefully. "You worked at Parasupe, right? What did you do there? If you don't mind me asking."

"I worked internally. With network security."

"So, you're a hacker?" It was hard to imagine.

She gave a small shrug. "Sort of. But mostly I just kept the network safe so no one could penetrate our system. Of course, to do that"—her lips curved up in a little smirk—"I needed to understand how they did it."

He handed her the bottle of wine and watched her look around for a glass, then tilt the bottle to her mouth when her search came up empty. There were cups in his saddlebag he'd forgotten, but he found he liked watching her drink from the bottle. Or, maybe it was knowing her lips were touching the glass where his had just been. "Can I ask what happened?"

Lowering the bottle, she licked away a drop of wine from the corner of her mouth.

Kohl's upper lip twitched, his fangs quickly descending just from that tiny gesture with her tongue. He forced himself to focus. He wasn't here to get off. He was here to get information. That was all. Devon wasn't a woman he could fuck and never see again.

"I found out my boss and her minions were doing something they shouldn't have been doing."

"Something against company policy."

"Something against *my* policy." She took another drink. "And, technically, the company's. It was just...wrong."

He waited, giving her time to decide how much she should trust him. It didn't take her long, and his patience was rewarded a few seconds later.

"The company was created by the U.S. government to keep an eye on supernatural creatures, and to suppress any danger to humanity. To remove it from the equation if necessary. But *only* if it was absolutely necessary. We weren't there to play God." She brushed her hands off on her jeans and took another sip of wine before passing it back to him. "And after all, starting a war with vampires wouldn't exactly be conducive to keeping the general human population in the dark about who our neighbors really are, now would it?"

"I take it employees of the company weren't real concerned about that." It wasn't really a question. He knew damn good and well the company didn't follow what they preached. It wasn't made up of enforcers. It was made up of assassins.

Devon shook her head, and Kohl watched, entranced, as the breeze lifted her curls until they danced around her face. "No. They weren't. Not all of them."

"So you turned them in," he guessed. "And that's why you were at trial."

"At the time, I was in disbelief. And I was angry that anyone would take it upon themselves to just wipe out souls on a whim." She looked away, out over the water. "Now, I wish I'd kept my damn mouth shut."

"You did what you thought was right."

"I did it to get back at my boss for cheating on me."

Kohl frowned, thrown off by the confession.

Her fingers twisted in her lap and she shifted uncomfortably. "I was sleeping with the head of my department. But apparently I wasn't the only one. When I found out about it, I went to confront them in their office, and I overheard a conversation I shouldn't have. I turned around and went back to my desk to check out what I'd just heard. That's how I found out what they were really doing."

Heat rose within him, hot as blue fire. Whether at the thought of anyone hurting her, or the fact someone else had touched her intimately, he didn't know. But he was going to find this male who had taken advantage of her. After all, accidents happened all the time. "He was a fool."

Devon nodded. "Yes, *she* was."

His murderous thoughts didn't diminish because the lover who hurt her was female.

She continued her story, unaware of the murderous contemplations roaming around in his head. "I started digging into her files. Anything I could find or crack on the network—her emails, her reports, her private correspondence, everything. Some I had access to, some I didn't. But I didn't care. I found what I was looking for and made it look like I'd stumbled across it accidentally, and I turned her in. She was the one leading the hunt. So, I set up a meeting. My mom's best friend was involved with the creation of Parasupe, and her recommendation is how I got the job there. She's known me since I was three, and I knew she would probably be the only one who would believe me. As soon as I told her what I'd found, she was on the phone. Within an hour I was secluded in a room and put under protection. I told the lawyers I would testify, and I was kept under wraps until the court date. The trial took place in a closed court, and the public was told there was a breach within the company. Something to do with not following some serious environmental laws."

"She got exactly what she fucking deserved, Devon. Not all of us are monsters." Himself excluded. Not because he purposefully set out to hurt anyone, but because he couldn't control the beast within him.

Meeting his eyes for the first time since she began her confession, she smiled slightly. "She did. But she also ruined my life. As soon as the trial was over, she set out to destroy me from her prison cell. Before a week had gone by, my face was plastered all over social media, and not in a good way. In the inner circles of the company, I was blasted as a liar, a Supe-lover, a traitor to humanity. To the rest of the world, I had used my position in the company to carry out my own anti-environmental agenda. They even said I wasn't a citizen, that I was, essentially, a spy. Here to bring down this country all by my little old self. I couldn't go anywhere without being harassed. Death threats appeared almost daily in my mailbox, under my front door, and once I left my house in the morning to find "cunt" and a hangman's noose spray-painted down the side of my car." She paused, and took a deep breath. "I had to get out of there. So, I moved here to Austin. And I've been laying low ever since."

She looked up at him with a rueful smile. Her eyes widened. "Kohl? What's happening to you?"

He was gonna hunt down and kill every one of those motherfuckers, that's what was happening.

CHAPTER 6

Devon stared at Kohl, unsure if what she was seeing was actually *what* she was seeing. Light reflected off the surface of his face and right arm, much like the moonlight shimmered on the surface of the water. Jewel-like colors rippled across his skin in tiny waves that rose and fell into something that nearly resembled scales, but...not.

She blinked and looked again. Tilting the bottle in her hand, she read the label, wondering what the hell was in the wine. But all she saw were the normal ingredients and warnings.

When she raised her head to ask him straight out if he'd spiked her drink, Kohl's fangs were fully extended and bared to her view, and his eyes glowed with that strange golden light she'd seen earlier at the club. Was that normal for vampires? She'd never read anything about that in the files at work. Recorded observations said only that their eyes would go black when they were "emotionally charged or feeding."

"Kohl?" She tried unsuccessfully to keep the tremor from her voice.

He stood, the movement so sudden he was sitting in front of her one second and standing twenty feet away the next. With his back to her, he rubbed the back of his neck and stared out at the water.

Concerned, Devon stood also and went to him. Unsure what to do, she lightly touched his arm. "Kohl?"

He exhaled a short hard breath out his nose and let his head fall back, blinking up at the night sky. Then he dropped his hand from his neck and glanced over at her. "It's okay. I'm good."

She tried to lighten the mood. "Funny. You look awful."

He barked out a laugh. "I'll be fine. I just need a minute."

His fangs weren't quite as noticeable now, his skin appeared perfectly normal, and the glow was fading from his eyes. Devon linked her fingers together in front of her and turned to look out over the water. "Okay." She didn't say anything else, just stood there beside him, giving him the time he needed. Maybe she was trying to prove to him that she wasn't afraid of him.

Maybe she was trying to prove it to herself.

It was quiet here. Peaceful. Devon took a deep breath of the crisp, clean air, and let the gentle lapping of the water soothe her, and throw off the funk she'd put herself in by opening up old wounds. She'd thought, after all this time, she'd be able to tell her story without it affecting her as much, but she'd been wrong. Maybe she'd never get over it. Maybe she'd always be a pariah of society. She sighed again, glad she had no family, no close friends, who were hurt by what had happened. Not really. Her parents were both gone, and Devon had been an only child. The friends she thought she'd had had abandoned her when the scandal broke out. She was used to being alone. It didn't bother her. Much. And she had Frank. He was all the friend she could handle at the moment.

After a few minutes, she felt Kohl's eyes on her. Standing side by side like this, the top of her head barely topped his shoulder. It was kinda strange for a girl who was used to being as tall or taller than many of the men she met. She felt tiny beside him. Fragile. She wasn't sure she liked it.

"I'm sorry that happened to you because of us. Because of things like…me."

Surprised his thoughts were running in that direction, she frowned up at him. "It wasn't because of you. It was because they thought the fact that they were human gave them the right to decide who lives and who dies. They thought they were acting for God. Or that they were better than God. I disagree with that logic. Who are we to decide what souls should be allowed to live, or not?"

"Do you really believe I have a soul?" The words were hesitant, as though he were almost afraid to ask.

"Of course. We all have souls."

"Hmph. If I have a soul, then it must be damned."

"Why do you say that?"

"Because I'm a killer, Devon. I've done things. Fucked up things. Things I couldn't stop myself from doing. Especially when I was young. I can try to act differently. I can try to control it, and I usually can—now. But at my core, I'm a predator. A killer." He watched her closely. "Thou shalt not kill, right? So, if you're right, and I do have a soul, it must be damned."

His argument didn't hold for her. "Animals are killers. They hunt for their food, or just for sport. Even sweet little cats and dogs. I don't believe their souls are damned, because that's how God made them. It's an instinct for them and, I would imagine, for you. It doesn't make you bad. Or evil. Not when you're doing what you need to do to survive." Her voice rang with conviction, conviction that was real. She truly believed everything she'd just said. The Christian's judgmental and vengeful God was not the God she believed in.

His eyes were intense on her face, as though he was trying to see right through to her soul. It made her uncomfortable, and she twisted her fingers together self-consciously in front of her. His interest in her as a person was more than she was ready for. Hot, sweaty vampire sex she could handle. But not more than that. Not right now. Not with him. Forcing a smile, she said, "Should we get back to our picnic before the ants carry off my dinner?"

The spell was broken, and she watched as the tension visibly left his body. "I have them spray for ants."

She rolled her eyes. "Okay, then, how about we get back to dinner because I'm still hungry, and I don't want all of the trouble you went through to go to waste?"

"We can do that," he said. "But first..."

Devon blinked as he disappeared from her line of vision. A second later he was back. Music drifted to her from the direction of his bike. The song was slow. A bluesy, soulful mixture of country and rock she instantly fell in love with.

He held out a hand. "Will you dance with me?"

The old-fashioned gesture was out of place in this day and age...and completely endearing. Her heart pounding out of her chest, she took his hand and stepped up to him, her other hand finding his shoulder. Muscle moved beneath her fingers as he pulled her in close and tucked their joined hands against his chest, and she found herself swaying in perfect time to the beat.

She fit against him like a puzzle piece. "Who is this band?"

"They're called Lucero."

"I like them."

He rumbled a response, and his arm slid beneath her open jacket and tightened around her back. Devon closed her eyes and laid her head against his chest, happy to shut up for the moment and just enjoy the warmth of his body and the pleasure of being so close to him.

They danced in silence for a while, swaying to the raw twang of the singer's voice. She felt drunk. And it had nothing to do with the wine. Kohl's heartbeat was strong beneath her ear, and his big arms held her safe against him, shielding her from all of the messed up shit in the world. For that short time, there was no one and nothing else but the two of them, and Devon found herself wishing the song would never end.

Until it did.

As the last notes faded away and their dance gradually slowed until they were no longer moving, she went to step away. But instead of releasing her, Kohl slid his hand up her back until he reached her nape. Gripping a handful of hair, he tugged gently until she tilted her head back.

His eyes travelled over her face and locked on her mouth. "I want to kiss you."

Her breath hitched as she waited. But he just stared at her lips, his eyes bright with hunger.

Was he waiting for her permission? "You can kiss me, Kohl," she said.

His heart began to pound so hard she felt it vibrate in her

own chest. Or maybe that was her heart. It was hard to tell where he ended and she began at this point.

His upper lip lifted, flashing his fangs. A growl rumbled low in his throat and his hand tightened in her hair. But he still made no move toward her.

"Kohl, please kiss me." She tightened her hand on his shoulder and rose up onto her toes, bringing their lips closer. "Kiss me," she ordered.

That strange light came on behind his eyes until they glowed the color of amber. Releasing the hand he still held, he cupped his large palm against the side of her face. "So beautiful," he whispered. His head lowered inch by inch, until he was so close she could smell the sweet scent of the wine on his breath.

Devon's blood pounded through her veins, making her lightheaded. Her entire body clenched with need. Sliding her free hand around his back and up to his other shoulder, she pulled, closing the distance between them until his lips touched hers. He moaned at the contact, and she tentatively tasted him, running the tip of her tongue along his lower lip. He tasted like wine and wind and barely restrained passion. She wanted to break through that restraint, wanted to feel him unleash the animalistic lust she felt simmering beneath the surface. She wanted to feel like a woman desired by a man above anything and everything else.

Sucking his lip into her mouth, she bit him.

He released a growl of need and pulled her head away until she could see his face. "Are you sure this is what you want?" he asked her. "You see what I am?"

Devon met his glowing eyes. "I see you, Kohl. I've never wanted a man more."

He frowned at that. "I'm not a man, Devon."

"It doesn't change the fact that I'm aching for you to touch me." She wasn't lying. She did ache—her breasts felt swollen, her nipples overly sensitive. Heat pooled between her legs, and her loins felt heavy, raw lust rolling through her in waves. "Please," she whispered. "I want this. I just want tonight."

With a sound of surrender, he relaxed his grip on her hair and lowered his mouth back to hers. This time he kissed her with a need that matched her own.

Yet, he trembled with unleashed power in her arms. He was still holding back.

Linking both arms around his neck, she slid her tongue into his mouth, skimming his fangs to either side, and without thinking, she touched the tip of one with her tongue.

Kohl's fingers dug into her back and his entire body jerked against her. There was a brief sting of pain when his fang cut her, and she moaned. With a low growl, he sucked her tongue into his mouth, lifted her off the ground, and held her tight against him. He ravaged her mouth with his, kissing her with a desperation Devon felt all the way down to her bones.

And then, suddenly, he dropped her back onto her feet and pulled away.

Devon took a step toward him, but he threw both hands up in front of him, palms out. However, that didn't stop her as much as the predatory look in his eyes. Once more, she saw the skin ripple on his arms as he dropped them back down to his sides, his chest rising and falling with deep, ragged breaths.

"Stay there." His voice sounded harsh and the words came out sounding thick, like he was having trouble pronouncing the sounds.

Devon stopped. "Kohl? What's wrong? Did I do something?"

He shook his head, but kept his eyes on the ground.

Not knowing what else to do, Devon pulled her coat tighter against the sudden chill that ran through her.

After a few minutes, he scrubbed his face with his hands and raised his eyes to hers. The light was gone, but that didn't make them burn any less. "I'm sorry," he told her. "I lost control."

"So, is this..." She stopped. Tears blurred her vision. She didn't know why. She barely knew the guy. Devon cleared her throat. It was probably just a reaction from being so worked up only to come crashing down again. "So, is this something that can't ever happen between us, then?"

CHAPTER 7

That was a great fucking question.

And one Kohl felt the need to answer honestly. "I don't know."

She twisted her fingers together in front of her. A nervous habit he'd picked up on earlier. "I feel kind of stupid asking this, but...have you done this before? With women?" Her mouth twisted like she'd just tasted something sour. "With human women?"

He rubbed the back of his neck, trying to disperse the buildup of heat. "Yes."

She waited for him to say more, but he wasn't about to share the dirty details of a few sweaty, clumsy fucks that meant absolutely nothing to him. Less than nothing.

With a measured look she said, "And I take it you didn't have any problems getting up close and personal with *them*."

"No."

She startled, like his answer physically hurt her, blinking hard.

"But they weren't you, Devon."

Her eyes, which she'd hidden from him a moment ago, flashed up to his. "What does that even mean?"

Words rose within him. Words he couldn't stop. He was about to say too much again, but he couldn't suppress this outpouring of emotion any more than he could suppress what he was. "There's something about you...I don't know what it is. You haven't left my mind since I saw you that night on the news, when all that shit was going down with your old company. I saw what happened to you after, the witch-hunt that ensued. And I wanted so much to reach out and help you. But who the fuck am I? You don't even know me. Or, you didn't. And when I saw you last night at the club—" He laughed a bit self-consciously. "I thought at first I was imagining you. But I wasn't. You spoke to me. And then, I—" He paused. He'd almost forgotten she didn't remember most of what had happened that night. He stared at the grass at his feet, wanting to avoid the wariness that had to be written all over her face after he'd just confessed to practically stalking her.

But, no. Fuck that. She'd wanted to know what he meant. He'd followed her story, yes, but he wasn't about to become a creeper. If she couldn't handle it, then it would make that much easier to stay away from her after he'd found out all he needed to know. Kohl raised his chin with more than a hint of defiance, only to find her staring at him.

There was no wariness. No panic. Quite the opposite. The warmth was back in her eyes, along with a tinge of belief that he was out of his fucking mind. And she was probably right.

He inhaled, breathing her into his lungs, and made up his mind. "I couldn't let them hurt you," he finished lamely.

She frowned. "Let who hurt me?"

Kohl knew he was going to catch a world of shit for this, but she deserved to know. She *needed* to know. It was very possible her life was in danger. "The human men who infiltrated the club last night and shot up the place."

Uncomfortable laughter bubbled up in her throat, but it died again before it was fully developed. The smile faded from her face. "What are you talking about, Kohl?"

"You know what I'm talking about. They just forced you to forget."

"They who?"

"Hawke and Andrew. But it happened." He paused. *What the hell am I doing?* "I pulled you behind a tabletop as soon as I knew bullets were about to start flying. One nailed me in the hip, but I barely felt it. All I could think about was that you'd been through too much in your short life to die in some random shooting. And that was before I'd seen you really smile." His own lips turned up at the memory of the light that radiated from her face when she was happy. "You need to know. It wasn't a random shooting."

She held up a hand to stop him from talking. "Kohl, I don't—"

"Hawke spoke with you after it was over. He told Andrew to make sure you got home safely. I walked you out. We talked a little. You touched my face. And then Andrew wiped your memory and put you in a cab. He found out where you lived when you told the driver, and made sure your car was back at your place when you woke up."

She opened her mouth to say something, but closed it again. Her eyes widened as the color drained from her face until her skin was ashen. She swayed on her feet.

Kohl took a step toward her, but she held up her hand to stop him before he could touch her.

Kohl kept talking, watching her carefully as his words released the memories Andrew had locked away in her mind. Sometimes it was too much for people to handle. But Devon was strong. She would be okay. He told her more details, recounting everything that had happened, everything she'd said.

Suddenly, she winced and raised her fingertips to her temples. Her knees buckled, and she headed for the ground.

Kohl caught her, and helped her back over to the blanket. He helped her sit, remaining on his knees beside her. He sat back on his heels and waited.

She groaned and pressed her palms to the sides of her head. "What the hell is happening?"

"Your memories are coming back."

"Coming back? Where the hell did they go?" She winced at another wave of pain. "Wait. Don't answer that. Fucking vampires." Her eyes cracked open just enough to glare at him. "You didn't do this?"

"No."

"Why should I believe you?"

"Because I can't mess with your head like that. I can't read what you're thinking. And I can't make you forget things you'd be better off not remembering."

"But you're a vampire."

"I'm only half vampire." Shit. He hadn't meant to say that.

She looked at him with a question on her lips. One he wasn't prepared to answer. Luckily, he was saved as the last remaining wall in her mind came crumbling down and the memory of the shooting slammed back into her awareness with the force of a train. He knew exactly what it felt like, because it had happened to him before.

"Oh my God." A sob caught in her throat and tears filled her eyes, overflowed, and ran down her face. "Oh my God!"

Kohl reached for her. "It's okay, Devon. You're okay." Pulling her into his arms, he tucked her head against his chest and held her tight against him while the horrors of the evening before returned. This time, she didn't have the buffer of being in shock. Or the whims of a vampire to keep her calm.

He held her shaking body, absorbing as much of the terror and sorrow as he could, hating what she was going through, but not sorry he'd done what he had. Her emotions tore through him, rousing the beast with their intensity. Kohl gritted his teeth and held fast, determined to be there for her. After all, it was his fault she was going through this. He could have left her blissfully in the dark about it all. But somehow, that just didn't seem right. So, he held her, and fought back the beast when it stretched its wings and screeched with the need for vengeance.

When her sobs had diminished to an occasional sniffle, and her emotions were so used up and wrung out he barely felt them anymore, she wiped her face on the sleeve of her coat and sat up. She didn't move away from him, though, and he felt a rush of male satisfaction that she trusted him enough still to allow him to continue to comfort her.

Red, swollen eyes searched his face as her hands gripped his forearms. "You came out of nowhere and knocked me to the floor." She paused. "You saved me."

"I did." An uncharacteristic sense of pride wound through him.

Devon studied his face for a long time. Kohl knew what she

was seeing, but it was okay. He had it under control. However, he couldn't turn it off, or barricade himself from what she was feeling, even if he wanted to. His mixed blood made him so much stronger in some ways, and so much weaker in others.

When it got to be too uncomfortable, he started to turn away, to hide his fangs and his eyes and his crawling skin, more out of habit than anything else, but then he stopped. He was what he was, and it wasn't anything she hadn't seen before now.

Reaching up, she touched his face much as she had the night before. Her hand trembled, but her voice was strong. "Thank you for what you did for me."

"You told me that last night."

"I'm telling you again."

He brushed her hair from her face. "You're welcome." Then he handed her a napkin.

Devon dried her face and blew her nose. Spotting the wine bottle, she picked it up and took a big swig before speaking again. "Why are you doing this? Making me remember?" Her face twisted in disgust. "Your friends obviously thought I didn't need to." She watched him closely for any kind of reaction. "I guess they must have had their reasons. Though I seriously doubt it was out of any concern for me."

He chuckled at that. "No. That wasn't the reason." Then he shrugged. "You were the only human left alive. It's a safety precaution. One I had to go along with to ensure you stayed that way."

She froze with the wine halfway to her mouth. "Is my life in danger now? Because I know?"

"Not from my coven. They won't know you remember unless I tell them, and I sure as hell ain't about to do that." He rubbed his eyes with one hand. "I shouldn't be telling you any of this."

"Is there more?"

Kohl didn't respond right away, wishing like hell he could tell her no.

She saw the way he was looking at her and took another large drink of wine. "Just do it. Lay it on me."

Kohl took a deep breath. "Those guys that shot up the club, they weren't after the coven. At least not only us. We think they were there for you, Devon."

She stilled. "How do you know that?"

"Mark, our bouncer that night, found one of them still alive. He compelled him to tell him who they were. The guy told him he was there to kill you, but he died before Mark could find out who sent him." He put his hand over the center of his chest, trying to contain the ice-cold fear that came from saying it out loud. His and hers combined. "They were after you, Devon. And you need to know this because there might be more coming for you. You're in danger, and you need to watch out for yourself."

"Who the hell would be after me?" Her eyes shot back to his. "Parasupe?"

"We don't think it was them. These guys were amateurs."

She pushed herself to her feet and walked a few feet away. Arms crossed over her chest, she shook her head. "It doesn't make sense. Who else would want to kill me?"

Kohl stood as well. "Is there someone you're close to? A friend? A family member? A—" He couldn't say it, couldn't even think she might have a lover. "Anyone else you're close to that can maybe stay with you during the day? Devon?"

She spun toward him, her anger hitting him square in the

chest. "I'm staying under the radar. I'm keeping my head down. I work in a pottery shop and I make deliveries for extra cash, for Christ's sake. I don't even own a computer! Who the hell would do this?"

"I don't know."

"It doesn't make any sense." She started chewing on her thumbnail. Then she shook her head. "No. I think you're wrong. There's something else going on. Why would anyone be after me?"

Kohl wished he had an answer for her. But no matter how many times she asked the same question, he just didn't know.

"And why would they kill all those people, " she said more to herself than to him. "Just because I was there?" She shook her head, saying again, "It makes no sense." Tears slid down her already damp cheeks and distance held her eyes. "It was a complete slaughter."

Kohl didn't bother to tell her that the vampires who owned the club had probably taken out a few innocents themselves in their quest to take out the shooters. And most likely it had been done on purpose. No witnesses meant no questions. If it had been the Master who had come up and not Hawke, Kohl had no doubt in his mind Devon would not be here with him right now, either.

The beast stirred at that thought, and a pulse of anger shook his bones. It appeared he wasn't the only one feeling protective of her. But he didn't have time to consider the implications of this. "Devon, why don't you stay with me until we figure out what the hell's going on?" Once the words were out, he couldn't take them back. The coven would never allow it. But, dammit, he didn't feel comfortable leaving her alone at her apartment with no one there to watch out for her.

She wiped the moisture from her cheeks. "That's not necessary, Kohl. And probably the most horrible idea you've had so far. But thank you for offering."

He took her hand. "I can't just drop you off at your place and leave you there."

"Why not? You barely know me. You've got no skin in this game."

The beast rumbled within him and he flashed his fangs. "Don't do that."

"Do what?"

"Push me away."

"Why shouldn't I?" She pulled her hand from his.

Her tone was cold, but he knew it was only a defense mechanism, because he felt her desperation to be near him even as she said it.

"And really," she continued. "Why wouldn't you want me to at this point?"

Her question made him pause. Why wouldn't he?

He ran a hand through his hair. She was right about one thing. His suggestion was crazy. There was no way he could take her back to the coven. Even if by some miracle he could talk the Master into it, he'd never be able to leave her alone. Not without worrying he would come back to find her cold and drained and thrown in a heap in a corner somewhere. Sneaking her in was out of the question, they'd smell her as soon as she entered the caverns, if not before. He exhaled. "Fuck. You're right. I can't take you back with me."

She sighed heavily. "I'm sorry." Then she took his hand with both of hers. "I appreciate your concern, but I'll be okay, Kohl. I have a friend across the hall. I'll let him know what happened. He's at my apartment or I'm at his most of the time anyway."

Kohl suppressed the surge of possession that rose within him. One kiss did not mean he had any claim on this gorgeous woman. He was here to get information from her, and he'd done that. He would take what he'd learned back to the Master, and maybe they could figure out why the shooting had happened. In the meantime, he'd do everything he could to make sure she didn't become a target for the vampires as well, and could continue to live her life in peace.

Something inside of him twisted painfully at the thought of never seeing her again, but it was for the best. For both of them.

However, tonight, she was still with him.

The breeze picked up, and he brushed loose tendrils of hair from her eyes. "I want to kiss you again." The confession came from the truest part of him.

There was a sharp intake of breath, a loaded pause, and then Devon practically threw herself at him. He caught her in his arms, feeling her excitement and her desperation as intimately as he felt his own. Her desire flooded through him, heating his blood. She wanted him as much as he wanted her. His muscles tightened and swelled, his fangs descended, and his cock threatened to bust through the zipper of his pants. From one second to the next he went from wanting to kiss her sweetly to wanting to force her onto her hands and knees in the damp grass and ripping her jeans from that ass so he could be inside her.

Of course, he would do no such thing. Would never treat her that way. He just wanted a kiss. Just one more taste of that luscious mouth…

His entire body shuddered as he cupped the side of her face and lifted her lips to his. The first touch was sweet, vulnerable.

Kohl pulled away just far enough to search her face. He knew what he must look like—fangs, glowing eyes, sharpened features—but it only seemed to excite her more.

Her heart pounding fast and hard, she pulled his head back down to hers and Kohl returned her kiss with a moan of surrender. Lips and teeth and tongue clashed and dueled as the beast purred with pleasure deep within him. Her scent filled his nose. Her taste filled his mouth. And her curves filled his hands until there was nothing else but Devon.

Devon reached between their bodies and found him. His hips bucked forward, his cock swelling beneath her touch despite the restriction of his pants. She rubbed her palm up and down his length, squeezing when she reached the head that rose above the waistline. Rubbing her thumb over the top, she spread the drops of moisture that had accumulated in his excitement.

Kohl broke off the kiss and threw his head back, baring his fangs to the night sky as she worked him higher and higher. Her touch undid him, even through his pants, and too soon, he had to grab her wrist and stop her.

"I want to touch you," she whispered with ragged breaths. "I want you to touch me."

His upper lip lifted, his fangs tasting the air for the scent of her blood even as he shook his head. But he didn't release her. Rather he pulled her back in for another kiss, holding her hands trapped behind her. He couldn't handle her touching him like that again. Not if he wanted to have any chance of getting her home unharmed. But he wanted this moment. He needed this moment.

So, he kissed her. He kissed her until the scent of her blood and the taste of her mouth was the only thing in the world. He kissed her until he felt every inch of her body and yet he couldn't get close enough. He kissed her until the beast was fully awake and stretching its wings, watching with interest.

He kissed her until he was forced to stop.

With one last touch of his lips on the corners of her mouth, he touched his forehead to hers. They stood that way, breathing the same air, his hard body weeping with disappointment, until he could speak somewhat coherently. "I need to take you home."

Devon pulled away just enough that she could look up at him. "I don't want to go."

An ache filled the center of his chest. "I don't want you to go. But you have to."

She took a deep breath. Eyes filled with disappointment, she stepped back.

He was glad she was the one to break the connection, because honestly, he didn't think he was capable, in spite of his insistent words.

They packed up the picnic in silence, eyes full of longing catching and holding every now and again. Then Kohl drove her home, taking the back roads to prolong the feel of her body pressed against his back and her arms tight around his waist. When they reached her apartments, he walked her to her door and watched her walk in and turn on her lights. Assured no one else was there and she was safe, he made her promise to keep her door locked and though he knew he shouldn't, he gave her his cell phone number with instructions to call if she so much as saw an unfamiliar face anywhere near her place. Then he waited as she shut and locked her door.

Kohl stood outside her apartment all of two seconds before he knocked twice.

She opened the door immediately.

"Can I see you tomorrow night?"

A dazzling smile lit up her face. "Yes." Then she shut and locked the door again.

He went back to his bike and headed home. He'd fill in the Master tomorrow night. Tonight, he was keeping her to himself.

CHAPTER 8

Devon stopped at the store to pick up a few groceries and made it back to her place with lots of time to get ready for her date. All she needed was a shower, a change of clothes, and a little sweet almond oil on her hair when she took it down to refresh her curls. She used to spend a lot more time and money on her hair, but with her recent "fuck it all" attitude she'd adopted, she'd let it grow out natural for the first time in...longer than she could remember. And she was surprised to discover she really liked her own hair.

A bag in each arm, she climbed the stairs to her second floor apartment and entered the interior hallway. Her place was about halfway down, and as Devon approached, she slowed her steps. Her door was partially open.

She stopped where she was and set down her bags. Pulling her phone out of her purse, she called 911. An operator answered. Calmly, she told her who she was, where she was, and why she was calling. The woman dispatched a patrol car and asked Devon to stay out of her apartment and on the line until they got there.

Frank appeared from the stairwell, a basket of laundry in his arms. He silently questioned her with both eyebrows raised when he spotted her standing in the hallway talking on her cell.

Devon pointed toward her door, still talking to the 911 operator. Cupping her hand over the bottom of her cell, she asked Frank, "Did you see anyone go in or out of my apartment while I was gone?"

He shook his head. "Your door was shut when I went down to the laundry mat."

"How long ago was that?"

"About twenty minutes? Just long enough to get my clothes out of the dryer and fold them."

She relayed the information to the operator who called it in to the squad car on its way. The operator then told her to take her friend and leave the building until the police showed up, so she grabbed Frank and dragged him back out to the stairwell with her, leaving her groceries in the hall. Hopefully, their other neighbors would stay in their apartments.

When they got outside, he set down his basket. "What the hell's going on, Dev?"

"I think someone broke into my apartment. The door was open when I got home just now."

"Are they still in there?"

"I don't know. I called the police as soon as I noticed it and then you came in."

Frank looked up at the building. "Why the hell would someone break into these apartments? They gotta know we are the brokest motherfuckers in Austin. At least on this side of the highway."

Devon had a good idea who it was, and it had nothing to do with how much money she made—or didn't make—and everything to do with what had happened at the club. Swallowing down the rush of horror and mourning that had kept her up most of the night, she just shrugged. "Here comes a police car."

She and Frank spent the next twenty minutes giving their statements while a female officer went up to check out her place. She came back outside ten minutes later and gave them the thumbs up that it was all clear.

"Okay," the officer who was taking her statement said. "Let's go up and have you take a look around. See if anything is missing."

Devon nodded and led the way back to her apartment, even though she knew in her gut everything would be just as she left it. They weren't after her stuff. They were after her.

Frank gave her a kiss on the cheek and took his clothes in to put them away after making her promise she'd come get him when the police left.

Devon opened the door to her place and went inside, the two officers close on her heels. It took her all of about two minutes to look around and confirm that everything was exactly as she'd left it. Even her money stash, in a spot that was quite obvious for anyone who knew where to look, was still there. All seventy-nine dollars of it.

She smiled at the officers. "Everything is here. Maybe I just didn't shut the door all the way." Bullshit. Devon always made sure the door was closed and securely locked. "I'm sorry to waste your time."

"No apologies necessary, ma'am," the male officer said. "We'd always rather be safe than sorry, as the saying goes."

"Yes, sir. Thank you again." She shook their hands and showed them out, waiting until they were in the stairwell before she went to get Frank.

He opened the door, and a cloud of skunky smoke preceded him out.

"It's safe now," she told him as she waved her hand in front of her face. "You can come over."

"Thank God. I hate cops."

"And yet that doesn't stop you from lighting a joint when they're right across the hall."

"It wasn't a joint. It was my bong. And I told you, they make me nervous." He closed Devon's door behind him and went straight to her fridge. "So, who's breaking into your apartment, Dev?" He peeked over his shoulder. "And don't bullshit me. I know you know. Or at least have an idea."

She sat at the table and started tracing circles in the condensation left by her glass of iced tea earlier, and decided to tell him. She needed to tell him. If for no other reason than so someone would know if anything happened to her. "Remember yesterday when I was so hung over from going dancing Thursday night?"

"Yeah." He found a jar of peanut butter in her pantry and brought it and a spoon over to the table, sat down, then immediately hopped back up to get a glass of her tea. "What about it?" he asked when he got back to the table.

"I wasn't hung over. At least, not from drinking. I went to The Caves."

Frank nearly choked on his peanut butter. "What the fuck, Devon? Why did you go there?"

She swirled her finger in the ring of water, strangely calm. Frank was one of the few people who didn't work at Parasupe who knew the same things she did about the owners of that club. Because she'd told him after she knew him well enough to know that in spite of his frequent ridiculousness, she could completely trust him. And, she wanted to make sure he knew what he'd be getting himself into if he were ever invited there. "I don't know why I went there. I just wanted to be around people, without being around people. You know?"

He snorted. "Uh, yeah."

"Honestly, I just needed to get out of this box, and you weren't home, so I just started driving, and somehow I wound up there."

"I need bread." Frank got up and went back to her pantry.

"There was a shooting while I was there."

The pantry door slammed. Frank spun around, a loaf of bread in one hand and a jar of dill pickles in the other. "Holy shit. Inside the club?"

"Yeah."

"How many shooters?"

"I don't really know. Two? Three, maybe."

"Who the hell would do…" The words faded away as he saw her face. His neck reddened the way it always did when he was angry. "Son of a bitch."

Devon sighed and got up to get a towel to wipe up the water on the table. "Yeah."

"How many people?"

"Everyone on the dance floor." Her voice was thin. She cleared her throat.

"Just the humans?"

She shook her head. "No. Human and vampires, both."

"Definitely your old company."

"Sounds like it. But I'm not convinced. Why would they do something like that?" She stared at her friend, searching for an answer he couldn't possibly have. "The vampires said one of the shooters told them they were after me, but it wasn't Parasupe."

He came over and wrapped his arms around her—bread, pickles, and all—and hugged her tight. "I'm so glad you made it out of there, Dev."

She hugged him back hard. "Me, too. I was lucky. One of the bartenders saw it happening before any of us slow humans comprehended what was going on and knocked me out of the way." And then she lost it completely. She thought she'd cried herself out last night after Kohl had dropped her off. She was wrong. Once again, the terror and sorrow and outright rage of seeing and hearing people mowed down by bullets hit her full force. Their screams rang in her ears and the pungent smell of blood and fear filled her nose.

Frank held her the entire time. When her sobs turned to sniffles, he asked, "Do you think the shooters were really after you?"

"The vampires think so," she told him as she went for the box of tissues on the counter. Blessedly numb again, she wiped her face with trembling hands. "Come to think of it, I'm not sure why they let me leave. Though they did wipe my memory before they stuck me in a cab."

"Then how do you know this happened?"

"Because I remembered last night." She peeked up at him from beneath wet lashes as she grabbed a hand towel and wiped the table dry. "With a little help."

One eyebrow went up. "A certain bartender, perhaps?"

"I went back to the club during the day yesterday. It was like my subconscious knew something had happened there, but there was just this big blank spot in my memory. And I knew I'd had nowhere near enough vodka to black out. So, I went back. The back door was unlocked and I went in. I just wanted to look around, see if anything jogged my memory. It's disconcerting not to remember hours of your life."

"For you, maybe," he said, slapping a pickle on his peanut butter sandwich. "I actually prefer it that way."

Devon laughed. She couldn't help it. All of the horror and stress and longing that had been fighting for the top spot in her emotional wheel for the past sixteen hours finally broke. She laughed until tears ran down her face and she could barely breathe.

While she had her second breakdown of the day, Frank calmly ate his disgusting sandwich, completely ignoring her.

And that made her laugh even harder.

But, eventually, the laughter lightened to the occasional giggle, which then disintegrated into soft sobs. God, she was a mess. Even Frank put down his sandwich and came over to hold her again.

"I'm sorry," she told him. "I don't know what's wrong with me."

"You've probably been in shock, that's what's wrong with you." He patted her back. "It's okay, my love. Just get it all out. You've been through a traumatizing experience. Anyone would be a little wacky right now. And then you come home to find out someone's been in your apartment—because I know damn good and well you didn't leave the door open. You're worse than my mother when it comes to locking doors."

Embarrassment took the place of her hysterics. Devon

wasn't a girl who cracked easily. "I'm sorry," she said again. "I'm okay now."

Frank pulled away and studied her for a few seconds. "Annnd, she's back. Good. Unlike a lot of gay men I know, I'm not good with girls and their emotions. I try to avoid them whenever possible."

Devon grabbed a tissue off the counter and wiped at her face. "Girls or emotions?"

"Both."

"As your one night stand record proves."

Picking up his sandwich, he took a bite and made a face. "This is really gross, yet strangely satisfying." Then he took another bite.

It wasn't until she'd chased him back to his own side of the hallway and got in the shower that she remembered she'd promised Kohl she'd call him if anything happened.

Well, there's nothing he could've done anyway. It's the middle of the day. And no one was here.

CHAPTER 9

Kohl checked his phone for the nine-hundredth and sixty-fourth time since he'd woken up. There was nothing from Devon. No calls. No messages. But that was good, right? It meant she was fine. He'd asked her to call him if anything happened, and she would.

But he was still worried about her. In his limited experience, humans were easily traumatized, and although she'd appeared okay when he'd dropped her off, he now wished he'd stayed with her a while longer. Just to make sure she was all right.

He'd been avoiding the rest of the coven since he'd returned last night, not wanting to give anyone a reason to question his whereabouts and take the chance the Master would hear he'd already seen Devon. Kohl wasn't ready to tell him everything, yet. Because he knew once he did, he'd have no reason to keep seeing her. And even though that was what needed to happen, it wasn't what he wanted. And also because he had a bad feeling that once the Master had the information he needed from her, she would no longer be necessary to him. And not being necessary meant you were just taking up space and air that could be used for someone who *was* necessary.

Kohl rubbed away the heat rising in the back of his neck, then went back to work on the drink order he'd been working on. He'd volunteered to cover for Andrew for a few hours while his friend went to see his favorite meal. Working kept his hands busy, and he'd hoped it would keep his mind busy, too.

But, yeah. Not so much.

This was insane, these...feelings he had for this woman he barely even knew. But no, that wasn't right. He did know her. Maybe not all the little details of her life, but he knew the kind of woman she was. He knew her heart. He knew her mind. And she was one of the good ones. She was worth all he could give and do for her.

Even if she never knew what those things were.

Unable to stand it anymore, he pulled out his phone and texted her.

Everything good? I'm running the bar, but I can get out of here in about an hour. I hope it's not too late.

She responded almost immediately.

Ready when you are. I'm starving.

Kohl frowned down at his screen, then texted back.

I was going to take you to dinner. A real one this time. But go ahead and eat if you're hungry.

Her answer brought on a swift intake of breath and a rush of blood to his groin area.

That's not what I'm hungry for...

When he didn't respond, she followed up with—

Sorry if that was too forward of me, but it's true.

And how he loved her honesty. Kohl quickly told her he'd

be there as soon as he could, and went back to work. But his head wasn't in it. As a matter of fact, his body wasn't, either, and he dropped more than one glass and mixed up three orders in the hour it took for Andrew to return. Good thing he didn't count on tip money to support himself.

Andrew returned in the nick of time, and as soon as he transferred the pending drink orders over to him, Kohl rushed out of the bar and down to his room to change from his white button-down and tie into a long-sleeved, black cotton shirt. He didn't bother changing the black jeans and boots he was wearing.

As Kohl was going out, Jaz opened the door that led to the club, coming in. He stepped inside the caverns and stopped, letting the door swing shut behind him. Pulling the soda straw he was chewing on out of his mouth, he whistled. "Hoo-ee! Look at you! All in a hurry. Where ya goin', Kohl?"

It appeared Jaz was in a talkative mood. An occasion that was rare, and Kohl forced himself to slow down. "Just going to hang out with a friend. How are you doing?" Luckily, Jaz hadn't been inside the club when the shooting went down, but Kohl still felt the need to check in with him.

Jaz smiled, baring his one good fang. "I'm good. I'm good. Except,"—his eyes widened like some sort of bad Charles Manson imitation—"I don't even know what you *are*."

"You know what I am, Jaz," Kohl said. Despite his best intentions, he was quickly getting bored with this conversation, and just wanted to get the hell out of there. They had this same discussion at least a few times a week. Jaz sensed something was different with Kohl, but his memory—or lack thereof—didn't always let him remember. Kohl always knew when it was happening, because he would feel the vampire's eyes on him everywhere he went until, eventually, Jaz would come ask him.

Jaz's long, black hair fell forward to partially cover his smirk as he scuffed the floor with the toe of his biker boot. "Maybe I do and maybe I don't. I think you just don't trust me. But the Master trusts me, and he sent me to check in with you about our little witness the other night."

Kohl found that hard to believe. More like Jaz overheard something and couldn't stand being left out, so he'd taken it upon himself to check in on things. "I'm a vampire. Just like you." He paused. "And you can tell the Master I'm working on it." He went to walk around him, then stopped. "Actually, I'll tell him myself when I see him." Jaz probably wouldn't remember this conversation, anyway. Shouldering past, he went back into the club, around the bar, and down the opposite hallway.

Out back, he pulled his bike out of the storage garage where he kept it. Texting Devon to tell her he was on his way, he hit the throttle, spraying gravel in every direction as he finally got out of there and on the road to Austin.

Run-ins with Jaz were always disturbing. He wasn't sure what it was. Maybe because Jaz always seemed nervous around him, like he was afraid of him, even though Kohl had never so much as raised his voice with him. It wasn't the vampire half Jaz was afraid of. It was the beast. And he was right to be afraid. It only left ashes and scorched destruction behind.

He was a selfish bastard to bring that thing anywhere around Devon.

Kohl shut those thoughts down. He couldn't think about what he was doing too closely. He couldn't. Because if he did, he would turn his Harley around and go back to the caverns.

Instead, he let the cold wind suspend any doubts he might have, and before he knew it, he was pulling into her apartments.

He smelled it as soon as he entered the interior hallway—spearmint gum and the faint stench of lead—and it got stronger the closer he got to Devon's door. Along with a scent that hadn't been there before. A male. Human, from what he could tell. Without bothering to knock, he opened her door and stepped inside.

The scent was very strong now.

"Devon? Devon!"

She came out of her bedroom, dressed in a gray-blue sweater and black leggings with a pattern in the same color. Combat boots were on her feet, and her hair was down. Her naturally sweet scent was mixed with something like almonds, and Kohl was temporarily distracted from the hunt as it wafted over him, but not for long.

She smiled at him, and then frowned. "How did you get in? Hey, did you break my lock?" Her tone wasn't quite angry, just a bit annoyed.

Kohl shook his head. "Who was in your apartment today?"

"What?"

"Who was in here? Was there a maintenance guy here or something? Cable guy?"

She walked past him and checked her door.

"It wasn't locked, Devon."

"It wasn't?" She closed the door and locked it, then turned and slapped her palm against her forehead. "Oh, that's right. Frank."

"Who is Frank?"

"My friend. The guy who lives across the hall."

Kohl ignored the burning ache in his gut. "No. That's not it. I know that scent. Who else was in here?"

Her hands tangled together in front of her. "The cops."

"Cops?"

"Yes. Well, one cop. A woman. I ran to the store earlier and when I got back my door was cracked open. She came up and checked to make sure they were gone before I came back inside." She crossed her arms. "I know I didn't leave it open. I always lock my door."

"It was unlocked just now," he pointed out.

"That's because I was distracted." She licked her lips, drawing his eyes, and then she looked away. "Frank was here and we were talking and I got upset. I couldn't stop laughing. And then I couldn't stop crying. Or vice versa. And then, well, then Frank left and I went to take a shower." She looked up at him. "But normally, I lock my door. I always lock my door. I'm anal about it."

"You told your friend what happened?"

She lifted her chin, as if she were expecting to be reprimanded for it. "I did. I thought it would be good for him to know, in case something like this happens again, or he sees an unfamiliar person wandering around. He'll know to pay attention."

"You trust him?"

"Completely."

Kohl nodded. If she trusted the guy, that was good enough for him. Restless, he paced around her apartment, following the scent right into her bedroom. He took in the practical dresser and full-sized bed, covered in a plain, white comforter with colorful pillows thrown against the headboard. The scent was strong in here, and the beast stirred at the thought of a strange man infiltrating her private sanctuary, going through her drawers and closet, and dirtying that white comforter doing God knows what.

And it wasn't the fucking cops. There were two separate unfamiliar scents. One female. And one male.

Kohl glanced back at the bed, closer this time. He could see the indentation of his form, and he ran a hand over it to smooth it out, barely resisting the urge to rip the blankets and sheets off her bed and throw them out the window. A deep growl fired up from his gut. He came back out and went into her bathroom. The fucker had been in here, too. Probably pissed in her toilet.

"Kohl? What is it?"

"Was anything missing? Did you check?" Rubbing the back of his neck, he joined her in the living area where she waited patiently.

Devon nodded. "I did. Nothing is missing." She came to stand in front of him, and a look of concern crossed her features as she studied his face.

"Why didn't you call me?" And there it was. The real reason he had this sick feeling in his gut.

"It was the middle of the afternoon—"

He slashed his hand through the air. "It doesn't matter. You promised you would call me if anything happened."

She took a step back and her hands went to her hips, steel glinting from her eyes. "And what the hell would you have done, Kohl? Huh? Run out into the sunlight to come and save me? Like I was some sort of damsel in distress? You wouldn't have made it two feet."

"I would've done something."

"What exactly would that be?"

He would've shifted and flown over here, and fuck the witnesses. "I don't know!"

Her eyebrows rose at his tone.

Kohl reined in his temper. He wasn't angry with her. He was angry at the thought that something could've happened to her and that she was right. There wasn't a fucking thing he could've done about it. He scrubbed his face with his hands. "I'm sorry. I just…I'm worried about you." Biggest understatement of the year.

Her fingers wrapped around his forearms and pulled his hands away from his face. She smiled up at him, and the spark of life lighting up her eyes chased away his fears. "I'm fine. I didn't come in. I called the police. And Frank came over and hung out with me for a while after they left, just in case. At least until it was time for me to get cleaned up for our date. And speaking of which—" She laced her fingers with his. "I seem to remember a certain someone promising me dinner."

Kohl stared down at their linked hands. His large and inked, hers elegant and soft. They were the prettiest hands he'd ever seen. He took a deep breath and raised a hand, still linked with hers, to touch her face with the tips of his fingers. "I did. Are you hungry?" He grinned. "For food?"

She laughed up at him. "Actually, I really am starving. And I would love to go have dinner with you. But,"—worry lines appeared between her eyes—"won't that be weird? For you, I mean. To just sit there while I eat?"

"No. It won't be weird. I'll have some wine. Doesn't do much, but it doesn't hurt." He dropped a kiss on her knuckles, wishing they could stay in, but knowing it wasn't going to happen, much as he would like it to. This woman affected him too much.

There were times, when he was with others, the vampire in him made an appearance. It was hard not to. Feeding and sex were closely linked for him, one enhancing the other. But no woman he'd ever been with had awoken the beast. Not ever. Not until Devon. However, last night, he'd felt the beast stretching its wings both times he'd kissed her. Felt its pleasure. Almost as if, every time he touched her, he had to share her with the thing inside of him. It both unsettled and infuriated him. Kohl didn't like to share. "Are you sure you're doing okay? You look tired."

She shrugged. "I didn't sleep much last night, but I'm glad you're here."

Her words warmed his heart. "Is Irish food okay? I know this great little place on the outskirts of the city. It's small, but this great family owns it, and it's never crowded. Even on a Saturday night."

"It sounds perfect. Let me get my coat."

While he waited, he glanced around her place again, wondering if she'd agree to have cameras installed, at least out here in the main room.

They took her car this time, as the temperature had dropped during the day and this night was much colder than the last, and the restaurant was a bit of a drive. Kohl gave her directions, and they talked more about her previous job and what she was doing to make ends meet now. It was easy to see she was wasting her intelligence, but she assured him she was content to have work where she didn't have to double guess every move she made.

Somehow, he didn't quite believe her, but he let it go.

They arrived at the restaurant, a little stone house with a green roof set back away from the road, and Devon gasped when they pulled into the parking lot. "It's just like a little cottage! How charming!"

Kohl got out and ran around the front of her car to open her door for her. "It *is* a cottage. A perfect replica of one you'd find in Ireland, and everything inside is authentically Irish. The dishes, the lace tablecloths and curtains…even the owners. And the food is all made from scratch." As they walked up the stone walkway, he filled her in on what little history he knew of the place. "The parents came over from Ireland in the late seventies, if I remember right. They opened this place and the entire family runs it. The original owners are gone now, but the kids—all, like, in their forties or so—have taken over." He opened the door for her and followed her into a small entryway decorated with photos of their guests over the years. Beyond the entryway was the first room of the cottage, filled with little tables covered in white lace tablecloths. Another room opened up through an archway to their right, and there was one more room toward the back near the kitchen.

A middle-aged woman in a flowered dress with a lace collar and coral lipstick greeted them. She was still pretty, with long dark hair and bright blue eyes in a fresh-looking face, and her soft voice had a lovely Irish lilt. "Hello, Kohl! How are you now?"

He smiled at her. Though he didn't frequent the restaurant for the food, he'd gotten to know the family who owned it rather well. They were good people who minded their own business. "I'm good, Margaret, thank you." With a nod to Devon beside him, he said, "This is Devon. Devon, this is Margaret. The eldest daughter."

Devon smiled. "It's very nice to meet you."

"Oh, and what a lucky guy you are to have such a pretty

date," Margaret told him with a twinkle in her eyes, then she turned to Devon. "He's never brought a lady friend here, I'll have ya know."

Kohl grinned back at her. "Do you have a private table?"

"Of course. Come with me." With a smile, their hostess grabbed a couple of menus and led them to the room at the very back of the house. The place was nearly empty. Only one other couple was there, and it looked like they'd already eaten and were enjoying an after dinner coffee. Seating them at a table for two in the far back corner, Margaret lit the candles in the center of the table and promised them her brother would be right over with some soda bread and homemade butter.

Devon looked around at the wallpaper with its little green flowers and then felt the lace of the tablecloth. Traditional Irish music with soft flutes played quietly in the background. She smiled at him. "This is so quaint. I love it, and I haven't even had the food, yet."

"It's quite an experience," he told her. "They're very into the presentation. Oh, and make sure you order the French Onion Soup if you like that kind of stuff."

"I love French Onion Soup," she told him.

Their server arrived, a man in his late thirties or early forties who looked much like his sister, only with shorter hair and a little extra girth, greeted them with the same soft, lilting voice and open smile. He took their drink orders and left.

Kohl watched the candlelight dance across the dips and hollows of Devon's face. The soft lighting did nothing to diminish the glow of her skin, and highlighted the shadows beneath her cheekbones. When she turned her head to the side to admire the knickknacks on the windowsill, the diamond stud in her nose sparkled prettily. But it was nothing compared to the glitter in her eyes when she looked at him. Kohl knew he was staring, but he couldn't help it. She was the most gorgeous woman he'd ever had the privilege to lay eyes upon. "Are you okay, Devon?"

Her eyes flicked up to his with surprise. "I'm fine. Why do you ask?"

"After what happened at the club the other night, I just want to make sure you're doing okay. We can leave at any time. Just say the word."

"Thank you." She gave him a small smile. "But this is nice. I really just want to not think about it."

He studied her. She really did seem all right. "Okay."

Their waiter came back with their wine and Devon ordered the soup Kohl had recommended along with the lobster dish, then handed the waiter her menu with a smile.

When he left, she picked up her glass and tried the wine. "Mmm. This is really good."

Kohl watched her lick a drop from her bottom lip, and his gums tingled, releasing his fangs just enough to taste the air.

Delicious scents came from the kitchen. It smelled good, even to someone like him. But not as good as the woman who sat across from him. The tantalizing aroma of her blood mixed with the earthy warmth of sunlight soaked into her skin was nearly enough to send him over the edge. He loved the smell of sunlight.

A sudden vision of Devon writhing beneath him, nude and warm from the sun, filled his head. The image was so clear he could feel her skin heating his.

"So, why can't you mess with my head?"

Her question took him by surprise and succeeded in distracting him from his lusty thoughts. "I'm sorry?"

"You said last night that you couldn't mess with people's memories. Is that true?"

"It is."

"Why not?"

They were interrupted by their waiter as he set down a basket of soda bread in the center of the table. Kohl thanked him and waited for him to leave before he answered her. "Uh… I just can't."

"But isn't that a normal thing for vampires?"

"Yes, but I'm not your normal vampire, Devon." Kohl's stomach churned. But not from hunger. This was not a conversation he wanted to get into right now.

"You keep saying that, but you've yet to explain what that means." She set down the knife she was buttering her bread with. "So, what does it mean, Kohl?" Her eyes bore into his, waiting for an answer, and if he didn't know better, he would swear she could see right through to the beast inside of him.

Fuck. He wasn't getting out of this, was he?

"And don't even think about trying to blow off my question again. I want to know who you are." She waved her knife at him. "Dammit, I deserve to know."

Nope. Not this time. "Devon—"

"Kohl, don't do that," she said quietly.

He was confused. He'd barely said anything. "Don't do what?"

"Don't patronize me. I can hear it in your voice and read it on your face. Just…don't."

She was right. She was absolutely fucking right. Kohl took a deep breath and gave her a nod. "I'm sorry."

Picking up her knife, she resumed buttering her bread.

Every few seconds, she'd shoot him a look while she ate, but she didn't ask again.

Lacing his fingers together on top of the table, he leaned forward.

She sat back and waited, eating her bread with a bored expression.

Kohl took a large drink of wine and tried again. "I'm only half vampire."

"And what's the other half? Human? Werewolf?"

"Kind of like that."

The bread landed on her plate so hard the knife fell off and landed on the table with a thud. "Kohl!" Glancing around, she lowered her voice. "Please. Just tell me. I'm not going to run away screaming. I know all about you guys, remember? Hybrids are rare, but they're not unknown to me." She took a deep breath and covered his hands with her own. "Please. I just need to know. I want to understand you."

The words began to pour out. "I can't fuck with your head because I'm only half vampire. My father was—is—a vampire. I don't know him. My mother...my mother came here from Iceland after she was publicly shamed for being with him. She got pregnant, and rather than drinking the herbs to rid herself of an unwanted child—a child she had no idea would survive or if it would be disfigured, or worse—she fought to keep the child and was banished. She came here to the states and the coven I now live with took us in. She had an old friend here." He paused. "She died when I was young."

Devon was staring at him with something akin to amazement lighting her features. "What is your mother, Kohl?"

He only hesitated a moment. "She was a shifter." And she'd

died before she could teach him how to deal with that side of his nature.

"From…Iceland."

"Yes."

Devon released his hands and sat back in her seat, staring at him in awe and something else he couldn't read. "Oh my God. That's not possible."

Kohl chugged down the rest of his wine. This is why he didn't tell anyone what he was. The only ones who knew the truth were Hawke and the Master. All of the others only knew he was a hybrid. They probably assumed it was wolf. He let them think what they wanted.

"Truly?" she whispered. A dawning look of understanding came over her face, and she sat up, her excitement washing over him. "That explains what I saw at the lake last night. Your eyes. And your skin."

"My skin?"

"Yes! On your arms. Like jewel-colored water rippling from your shoulders down to your hands." She suddenly stilled. "Oh, Jesus. Your skin…Kohl, you were turning."

"But I didn't," he said quickly. "I controlled it. I would never put you in danger by letting the beast out if you're anywhere near me."

Devon gave him a strange look. "The beast? Why do you call it that?"

His upper lip lifted in a disgusted sneer. "Because that's what it is."

She was shaking her head before he finished his sentence, her loose curls flowing around her face. "No. No, Kohl. Not a beast. A dra—" She cut off what she was about to say when the waiter returned with her soup. But as he set it down in front of her, she paid no attention to the shell of an actual onion sitting in a bowl with the soup inside, not even when he lit a lighter and flambéed it. Instead, she stared at Kohl through the top of the flames, and something about the sight of her, seen through the fire, seemed rather symbolic to him. But then they burned away, and the feeling was gone.

Uncomfortable being under such close scrutiny, Kohl smiled his thanks to the waiter as he presented her spoon on a tray. "You should try the soup. I hear it's really, really good."

Devon blinked. Taking the spoon from the tray, she smiled her thanks at the waiter. Perhaps sensing he was uncomfortable, she blew out the last lingering sparks and then dipped her spoon in for a taste. "Mmm. This *is* really good!"

Kohl relaxed as she dug into her food. Half of it was gone before she seemed to remember what they were talking about.

"I want to see it."

Kohl couldn't have heard her correctly. "I'm sorry?"

"I want to see it, Kohl."

Ah, if only she were talking about something other than the beast. "That's not possible."

"Why not?" She set down her spoon. "Kohl, do you realize how rare you are? I mean, come on. A dragon. You're a *fucking* dragon."

If there was one thing that would stay with him about this night and make him glad he'd told her, it was the fact that by revealing what he was, he'd managed to suppress the ever-present layer of melancholy that enveloped her spirit and saw—really saw for the first time—the strength of the light within her. His skin fairly burned from the intensity of it. And he despised himself for having to be the one to distinguish it again. "No, Devon."

She opened her mouth, no doubt to try to talk him into it, but then she paused, and really looked at him. Her eyes fell to the table and the animation left her face. With a sigh, she picked up her spoon, took a sip of her soup, then set her spoon down and sat back. That look was on her face again. The stubborn one. "Why not?"

Kohl leaned forward, closing the distance she'd created between them. "Because it's not safe for you. The beast has a mind of its own. I can't control it when it's released. The only thing I can do is try to keep it buried deep down inside where it can't hurt anyone."

"That must be difficult."

"More so when I was younger. The vampire side of me, now that's a little harder to hide. It's so easily stimulated." He smiled, showing her his fangs.

After a pause, Devon laughed, the melodic notes soothing him more than the music. He wished he could always hear her laugh.

"I really am sorry. I wish I could show it to you, if only to bring back the light in your eyes."

Her food came, and the conversation came to a halt for a few minutes while Devon ate. Kohl refilled their wine glasses, enjoying the sight of her pleasure with each bite of lobster wrapped in a flaky pastry. After a while, he changed the subject, talking about anything other then the thing inside of him. He asked her about her family, and found out her parents were both deceased.

"They were older when they had me. I was kind of a surprise, or so my dad liked to remind me. He said I was the best anniversary gift mom ever gave him." She smiled at the memory.

"What about brothers or sisters?"

"Nope. It was just me." She took a sip of her wine. "I was in college when my dad passed, and mom followed him a little less than a year later."

"I'm so sorry." And he meant it. Kohl had lost many people in his life. People he cared greatly about.

She gave him a sad smile. "Thank you. But I believe they're still together, wherever they are now. It's comforting. And I'm glad they weren't around when everything went down at Parasupe. My father would've been so furious. I would've had my hands full trying to keep him from trying to take out the entire company. It would've put all of us in danger."

"Your parents sound great, Dev." He reached across the table and took her hand, and as they stared at each other, the easy companionship they'd enjoyed throughout dinner was replaced by an electric tension that shot straight from their hands, up his arm, and straight down to his groin. It slammed into him with unexpected force, taking his breath and feeding his hunger.

Kohl was suddenly ravenous.

And by the way her eyes darkened and her lips parted, she felt it, too. "Are you sure you're not hungry?"

CHAPTER 10

Devon held her breath. Luckily, the words had sounded a hell of a lot more confident coming out of her mouth than they had inside her head.

Kohl tightened his fingers around hers for a few seconds, then he released her hand and sat back in his chair. He rubbed the back of his neck, his bright eyes never leaving her face. It was a habit of his, she'd noticed. Rubbing his neck like that. He seemed to do it when emotions were running high. But the average person looking at him wouldn't realize they were in the company of a hungry vampire. However, after only a couple of days, Devon knew him well enough by now to see the signs.

The brown of his eyes, though not gone entirely yet, had lightened a shade or two—something she now knew was caused by the shifter side of his nature. Specifically, his dragon. It made total sense now. His cheekbones appeared sharper in the candlelight. And if it weren't for his close-cropped beard, his jawline probably would, also. The muscles in his arms tensed and swelled beneath his long sleeves. He looked larger and harder overall, less relaxed, and if she looked very closely, she could see the tips of his fangs peeking out from beneath his mustache.

She wondered what they would feel like embedded in her throat. While working at Parasupe, she'd heard vampire bites could be quite pleasurable, especially if you were with someone who was experienced in that sort of thing. It didn't frighten her exactly, but she'd be lying if she said the thought didn't make her a "wee bit" nervous.

"Devon." His voice was deeper, raspier, and she knew he was just as affected by her as she was by him. He didn't say anything else, just her name.

"Let's get out of here," she said.

His eyes met hers, and his were pained. "I was sent to get information from you," he blurted.

It took her a minute to catch up with the change in subject. "What?"

"The Master of my coven ordered me to find you again and…get to know you, to get information out of you about your former company."

If he had thrown a bucket of ice water over her head, it would've felt warmer than the way she was feeling right now. "And you agreed?"

"I had to, Devon."

"Because he's your *Master*?" She couldn't keep the sarcasm from her voice if she'd tried. And she didn't try.

He flashed his fangs at her. "Because you would be dead right now if I hadn't."

She sat back in her chair. Hard. "Why? Why erase my memory and let me go if he was only going to kill me anyway?"

He scrubbed his face with one hand. "Hawke isn't the Master. He's the second oldest and his right-hand man, and much more rational than the leader of our coven. The Master is ancient, and very paranoid. And he doesn't like witnesses. Whether or not they remember what they saw."

She sifted through this new information. Though she wasn't happy about the fact he'd totally ruined the mood, she respected him for telling her now, rather than after he fucked her. "I don't really know what to say here, Kohl."

Leaning his elbows on the table, his eyes pleaded with her. "I just wanted you to know. I don't want to hide anything from you. Not with the way things are happening with us."

"Is something happening here?" She was beginning to wonder. Or was she nothing more than a convenient meal, and he was just playing his vampire games?

His eyes were filled with conviction when they caught and held hers, and there was no hesitation when he said, "Yes. Much as I would wish it otherwise."

Her heart began to pound. She knew he would hear it, but she didn't care. And there wasn't much she could do about it anyway. "I want to be with you, Kohl." She didn't know how much more blunt she could be. They could talk about everything else later.

"I want to be with you, too. But, I don't trust myself around you." He seemed to rethink that. "Well, not me, the vampire. I can control the thirst. The urge to bite. But I don't trust the beast. I'm afraid if we do this, I won't be able to contain him and I'll hurt you. Or worse."

Devon could see he truly believed that. But, somehow, she didn't. "But it's a part of you. If you have these—" She looked around, as though searching for the words in the wallpaper.

"Feelings for me, wouldn't the dragon within you feel it, too?"

"Honestly, I don't know, Devon. I've never felt this much for a woman before."

The words, spoken so matter-of-factly, threw her for a loop, and she laughed self-consciously. "You barely know me."

Reaching out, he took her hand. "That's where you're wrong. I do know you, Devon. I may not have been around until just recently, but I know your heart, and I know your soul. I can *feel* you, all the way down to my gut. I know you almost as well as I know myself."

Again, she was at a loss for words. Not because she thought he was out of his damn mind, but because she felt it, too.

Maybe they were both out of their minds.

The waiter came by to check on them and she asked him to wrap up the rest of her meal. Downing the remainder of the wine in her glass, she came to a decision. It was the craziest thing she'd ever done, but she wanted this man. Or vampire. Or dragon. Or whatever he was. She had no thoughts of the future, only of today. And she was tired of feeling sad. Tired of feeling like a pariah to society. Today, she wanted to take a risk. Life was too short, and as she saw just two nights ago, it could be ripped to shreds at any moment. She wanted this experience with Kohl. "I want to go back out to the lake."

He immediately started to shake his head no, but then he seemed to catch himself. "If we go out there, I don't know what will happen."

The uncertainty in his voice grabbed at her heart. "How about another dance? To start."

A slow, sexy smile lifted the corners of his mouth. "I think I can handle that." Fear clouded his expression. "And what about after the dance?"

The waiter appeared with her leftovers. Devon thanked him and grabbed her purse as Kohl paid the bill. "After the dance, if anything…happens. Then we'll be in the perfect place for that, too." She winked. "No witnesses."

CHAPTER 11

Kohl gave her directions to his property. Devon chatted the entire way about the different types of people she runs into working her delivery job and other inconsequential things. It was a welcome distraction from his own thoughts, which, he suspected, was exactly what she was trying to accomplish. He knew she was nervous, and just a little bit scared. But mostly, he felt her excitement. Honestly, he had to admire her for her courage. Not every woman would be willing to take on something like him. Not knowingly. But she was convinced that even if he shifted, he wouldn't hurt her.

He shifted his long legs, trying to get comfortable, and wishing he had her confidence. He should've asked to drive. He was too nervous and too fucking horny to just sit there beside her without having something else to concentrate on.

Every few seconds, he would check the side mirror. Something was eating at him. Something that had nothing to do with taking Devon somewhere they could be alone. He wasn't sure what it was, but it made the tiny hairs on the back of his neck and arms stand up. After checking the mirror a good ten times in as many minutes, Kohl decided he was just being paranoid. No one knew he was with her.

He glanced over at Devon, and he couldn't help but smile as she laughed. He had no idea what she was talking about, but man, he loved to hear her laugh. She turned back to the road, and as he studied her delicate profile, he came back around to thinking maybe this wasn't such a good idea. Every time he thought about being intimate with Devon, the beast stretched with pleasure, as eager as he was. But he didn't know if it was because it wanted to be with her, too, or if it just knew it would get a chance to come out and play if Kohl got riled enough. Though anything that heightened his emotions was enough to entice his vampire nature, the beast was never this close to showing up without an invitation unless there was severe danger to himself or those he felt protective of. Not since he'd learned to control his shifting, and that was a long time ago.

"What's wrong?" Devon kept her eyes on the road, but her hands tightened their grip on the steering wheel.

"Nothing. I'm good."

"No, you're not. You keep looking at the side mirror and your entire body is tense. Is there something going on? I haven't seen anyone behind us, but I keep thinking a bunch of guys with guns—or worse, sharpened fangs—are gonna drop out of the trees onto the roof of my car like in some movie."

"No. I'm just feeling kinda…unsettled." He rubbed the back of his neck. "I'm probably just being paranoid because this isn't supposed to be happening."

"Driving to the lake?"

"No. Us. Seeing you like this. I was explicitly told to stay away from you."

"I thought the coven Master wanted you to hang out with me. To find out what I know."

"He does. I was told to get information about what you did at Parasupe. But this—" He pointed back and forth between the two of them. "Was never supposed to happen."

She glanced at him for a few long seconds and then turned back to the road. "Kohl, I can't lie and tell you I don't want to be with you."

Her heart pounded, pushing blood through her veins. In such a small space, the sound was overly loud to his sensitive ears. It also heightened her scent, distracting him from her words. But then she reached for his hand, and the pressure of her touch cleared the haze. He wrapped his fingers around hers as his focus cleared, squeezing her hand.

"I'm not sure what it is, but ever since the night of..." She paused, and he felt, rather than saw, the myriad of emotions that threatened to overwhelm her as she remembered the night she'd first come to the club. She cleared her throat, and he felt her agitation diminish as she shoved it away. "Before we actually met, something kept drawing me back to that place. That night wasn't the first time I'd come there, just the first time I'd come in. At first I thought it was the secrecy of the club. The lure of going someplace where I could lose myself in the darkness. And then, I thought it was my mind trying to tell me it had been messed with after everything that happened. But I don't think it was either of those things. I think it's you. I think it's you I keep coming back to. And I don't know how, or why, but this is happening. This is happening with us." She glanced over at him. "Is that how it is with you, too?" She laughed, the high pitch giving away her nervousness. "Or am I just being a girl?"

Her confession threw him completely, and at the same time, he knew exactly what she was talking about. He'd felt this way since the first time he saw her on the news, only he hadn't known how to put it into words. This woman was now home to him. "Your blood knows me," he mused.

"What did you say?"

"Nothing. Just something someone said to me. Turn left up here." He pointed at the road ahead. "Yeah, right here."

A few minutes later, she pulled her car up to the end of the road. The water glistened in the moonlight as it rippled along the surface. Devon put the car in park but left the engine running.

"Your battery is gonna go dead."

She gave him a teasing grin. "Then you'll just have to fly me home."

Kohl touched her arm before she could get out of the car.

Her smile wavered when she saw he wasn't sharing in her playfulness. "It's okay, Kohl. I was just going to leave it on for a few minutes so we could play the radio. I wasn't kidding about that dance. You owe me."

He shook his head. "Devon, just…keep your keys in the ignition. If anything should happen, anything at all, you run. You get in your car and you get the fuck out of here as fast as you can. Go to the nearest secure building and get inside. Don't leave your car running, though. It will see it and know where you are."

"You," she told him.

He frowned at her. "What?"

"*You* will know where I am. Not 'it'. You."

He exhaled heavily. "Fine. *I* will know." He took her chin between his thumb and forefinger. "Promise me you won't take any chances. If I shift, don't be stupid enough to think I'll know who you are. Because I swear to you, I won't."

She lifted her chin, breaking his hold. "I am far from stupid, Kohl."

He rubbed his forehead with his fingertips. "I didn't mean…"

She released her breath on a loud exhale, the tension flowing from her body. "I know you didn't." Then she smiled. "Come on. You promised me a dance."

"Devon."

She rolled her eyes at his stern tone. "Kohl."

He just looked at her, trying to think of what he could say that would convince her of how serious this was. How serious *he* was.

Reaching out, she took his face between her hands, rubbing his beard with her fingertips before she leaned forward and lightly touched her lips to his.

His cock stiffened instantly, and a helpless sound left his throat. No part of her touched him other than her hands and her lips, and his body was reacting like he'd never had a woman before.

He wanted this woman with a ferocity that terrified him.

She released his face and turned the keys, shutting off the engine. Pulling out her phone, she swiped at the screen. A moment later, music played from the small speaker. Garth Brooks was singing about *The Dance*. Kohl knew the song well. And he knew after this night, it would haunt him whenever he heard it, because he was getting too close. This would be the last time he would see her. It had to be. And if he were any kind of gentleman, he would take her home right now. Take her home and never see her again. Tell the Master what he wanted to know, and carry on the way things were before he'd met Devon.

Apparently, however, he was no gentleman.

Kohl swallowed his frustration and fear and got out of the car, making it around to her side before she managed to get her door fully open. She froze for a second when he was suddenly there, before taking his outstretched hand and allowing him to help her out. She tossed her coat on the seat and shut the car door, bringing her phone.

He led her down to the lake, walking slowly to account for her lack of night vision, until the water lapping against the shoreline mixed with the country twang of Garth's singing. The air was colder than the previous night, but without a hint of moisture. But he knew it wasn't the cold that made her shiver when he pulled her into his arms and started to sway to the music in her hand.

Though she was tall, Devon's curves were soft, and fit against him perfectly. The loose curls on her head smelled sweetly of almonds and tickled his nose when he pressed his cheek against the top of her head. Lifting her hand to his mouth, he kissed the soft skin on the back, breathing in the warmth of winter sunshine radiating from her skin.

The beast stretched restlessly. It missed the sunshine.

Her chest rose and fell with quick breaths, her hardened nipples grazing his sensitized skin beneath their clothes. Her leg moved in and out from between his as they moved in time to the music, teasing him as his did her. He wanted to hold her like this skin-to-skin, without clothing as a barrier between them, and dance naked under the stars.

Neither spoke, each too absorbed in the feel of the other. He held her close, with just enough room between them so their bodies slowly teased each other with every step. Devon let him set the pace, and even though a part of him wanted to be inside of her five fucking minutes ago, another part was thoroughly enjoying the subtle seduction of the dance.

Soon, the rising scent of Devon's desire enveloped them, feeding Kohl's lust. Cheek to cheek, her breath was heavy in his ear as her fingers tickled the back of his neck. Kohl pulled her tighter against him, keeping her warm with his ever-increasing body heat. Fangs bared, he slid one down her jaw, careful not to break the skin. She shivered, tightening her arm around his neck and pressing closer to him. Kohl wanted like hell to absorb her into his skin, make her a part of him, so he would have the feel of her, the scent of her, the life of her spirit, with him always.

And still, they danced.

When his blood was racing through his veins so hot and heavy his cock felt like it was about to burst from his pants, and Kohl was convinced he wouldn't be able to breathe another breath without kissing her, he pressed his lips to the top of her head, then her temple, and then the corner of her brow.

Devon lifted her head from his chest and turned her face up to his. Her eyes were bright with desire, and he watched as the tip of her tongue wet her lips.

With a groan of surrender, he took her mouth with his. He kissed her like he would never have the chance again, while trying to ignore the truth that he most likely never would. He wanted to tell her how she affected him—what she meant to him—but for once, he found he had no words. So, he would have to show her.

Kohl tightened his arm around her hips and pulled her up into him, molding her against his hardness. He moaned at the taste of her mouth, the feel of her body, the scent of her blood and her lust for him. He knew if he touched her, she would be wet and ready for him, and once he thought it, he couldn't remove the image from his head. Sliding his hand down over her ass, he lifted the back of her sweater, exposing her bare skin to the cool night air and the heat of his palm. He found her bra enclosure, and realized his hands were shaking so much he could barely get it unhooked.

Devon sighed with pleasure when he finally got it and rubbed the spots where the elastic had made indents in her back. A low growl rose in his throat at the thought of anything marring that beautiful skin, even temporarily. Bras were torture devices for women, but better than the contraptions they used to wear.

He let go of her hand, wrapping both arms around her as she hung on to his shoulders. Lips, teeth, and tongues clashed as he filled one palm with her curvy ass, holding her hips against his to relieve the aching hardness of his cock, while the other palm skimmed her ribcage and made its way between their bodies. He hefted the weight of her bare breast, rubbing the nipple with the pad of his thumb.

Fingers digging into his shoulders, Devon moaned and arched her body, the movement breaking off their kiss as she fought for breath. His fang scraped her bottom lip, drawing blood. Looking right at him with eyes heavy with desire, she licked it clean.

Kohl flashed his fangs at her. He wanted to taste her. He wanted it so badly that if someone tried to get between them right now, friend or foe, he would rip them limb from limb to get to her.

And still, they danced.

CHAPTER 12

Kohl suddenly stiffened in Devon's arms, and not in a good way. But he kept dancing, turning her a little to the right.

Pulse racing at the sudden shift in mood, she studied his expression in the dim light from her phone. But other than his eyes shifting from side to side, a common observer would have no idea that anything was wrong. She dropped her eyes to his mouth. His fangs were exposed, but that wasn't unusual after what had just happened between them. There was no rippling of skin or other indications he was shifting. Seemed safe enough.

He suddenly looked down at her with such a desperate sense of wanting and loss, a wave of desire flooded her core, hitting her so hard it nearly buckled her knees. A split second later his expression hardened into a cold mask she'd only seen once before.

"What is it?" she whispered.

He didn't look around or make any other unexpected

movements, but she could feel the slight shift in his stance as he casually played with her hair with one hand. His eyes met hers as he shuffled his feet, turning her a little more toward the lake and removing his hands from beneath her sweater. She shivered in the sudden cold.

Heart pounding, she watched as his eyes gradually brightened until they were twin beams of light in the darkness—glowing tawny, then golden, then rose gold. The pupils changed—elongating and contracting until they were cut like slivers of diamonds. His upper lip lifted in a snarl, his fangs longer than she'd ever seen them, and beneath her hands, his skin felt loose, detached from the muscle.

Yet, somehow she knew this was not about her. Someone was here. His refuge was no longer safe. She tried talking to him, hoping she could still get through. "Kohl, you're scaring me."

"Keep dancing." His voice was a low growl, his words barely articulate. "But be ready to run when I tell you. Go straight to your car, stay out of the trees."

She noticed he'd positioned them as they danced so her back was toward the water and he was between her and whatever danger had found them.

"What's wrong?"

"They're here."

She leaned to the left and peered around his arm, her eyes skittering from the trees to her car. She saw nothing and no one in the glare of the headlights. "Who?"

Kohl pulled her closer against him, drawing her head into his chest, covering the side of her face with his hand. "Vampires." He took a deep breath, his chest rising and falling beneath her head. "Four, smells like." She felt his lips press against her hair. "I'm so sorry. This is my fault. I shouldn't have brought you here again." But before she had a chance to ask him what he was talking about, he loosened his hold on her. "You ready?"

She smiled up into his eyes even as adrenaline flooded her system.

"On the count of three, I want you to run as fast as you can. Don't look back. Don't stop. No matter what you see or hear. Run straight to your car and get the hell out of here. But don't go back to your apartment. Call your friend and have him meet you somewhere. I'll find you."

Her fingers dug into his biceps. Neither of them seemed to notice. "What about you?" Her voice was barely above a whisper, but she knew he'd hear her.

"I'll hold them off until you get away."

"I'm not leaving you, Kohl."

He chuckled without humor, the sound rumbling through his chest beneath her ear. "Honey, I can take care of myself. You need to do as I say. Please." The last word was strained.

Devon didn't like this plan. Not one little bit. But he was right. What the hell was she going to do against a group of vampires? She nodded once against his chest.

Lowering his head, he whispered near her ear, "One, two…go!"

Kohl spun her around and gave her a push in the direction of her car. Pumping her arms, Devon stretched her legs as far as they would go and ran like she'd never run before. The cold air burned her lungs, but she didn't stop. She didn't look back. Not even when she heard grunts of pain and screams of rage from Kohl. Not even when she heard the grotesque wet, sucking noises of muscle tearing, followed by the snapping and popping of bones.

Good God, he was shifting. Devon had seen camera footage of a shifter once when she'd accidentally walked into her boss's office during an investigation meeting. The girl on the screen was a werewolf, and the change from human to wolf had looked excruciatingly painful. The thought of Kohl going through something like that, only ten times worse because of what he was, brought tears to her eyes despite the danger she found herself in.

She didn't look when she heard answering hisses and growls coming from the copse of trees to her left. And she didn't stop when Kohl was suddenly quiet behind her. He'd told her he couldn't control the "beast" inside of him. That it might not even recognize her. Now was not the time to test that theory.

She was almost there.

Something large and brutal tackled her from the side. She went down hard, her arms pinned to her sides, unable to break her fall, and hit the ground with a grunt of pain. Her phone flew out of her hand as her attacker landed on top of her, pushing the air from her lungs.

The first thing she noticed was the moisture seeping through her leggings and sweater. A strange thing to worry about at a time like this. Gasping for breath, she kicked her legs and clawed at the grass, fighting to get away, even though she had nowhere near the strength of her assailant. But she wasn't about to go down without a fight. Her mother raised her to be a lady, not a damn victim.

She was flipped her onto her back, and Devon froze as she stared up into the dark voids of its eyes. The vampire hissed, baring one sharp fang, spittle running down its bottom lip. With an evil smile, it wrapped its hand around her throat and squeezed.

Devon clawed at its hands, trying to ease the pressure on her windpipe. She didn't recognize this vampire. It wasn't one of the coven she'd seen at the club that night. Not that it really mattered at the moment, but it was what her mind focused on, like the wet grass soaking through the back of her sweater.

A high-pitched screech hurt her ears and they both froze. Seconds later, the ground shook like the earth was about to split open beneath her. Her eyes watered. She couldn't see what was happening. She couldn't get enough oxygen. The world began to tilt and merge together. In a last bid attempt to get free, Devon renewed her struggles, knowing she was about to pass out.

Horrid screams tore through the air around her, followed by a blast of heat so intense her entire left side felt sunburned. The vampire's single-minded focus was momentarily diverted and he whipped his head around, his long hair tickling her face. His hold on her throat loosened just enough for Devon to suck in a resistant breath. She began to cough.

The vampire, eyes never leaving whatever he was looking at, released her with something that sounded like a curse and yanked her to her feet by one arm.

She staggered, falling back down to her hands her knees, her eyes glued to the dragon not a hundred feet away from them.

It stood nearly as tall as the trees around them. Granted, they weren't the tallest trees in the world, but still, they had to be a good twenty or thirty feet. Black wings stretched out wide to either side. Thin, leathery skin—interspersed with blood-red veins—stretched between the bones. With a rush of wind that battered everything around it, they swooped down against its body, and Devon saw they were tipped with lethal spikes that dug into the ground. A large reptile-like head was held low to the ground, pinning them where they stood with Kohl's glowing eyes. Blood dripped down one side of its face. The neck was long and protected with two rows of plated bone, as was it's sinewy back.

Standing on powerful back legs, a long, muscular tail with more spikes on the end whipped to the side as it opened its wide mouth and roared. When it moved, Devon saw its skin wasn't black at all, but multi-chromatic with jewel tones that shimmered in the moonlight. Three smoking piles burned between the dragon and them.

The remains of the other vampires.

"Motherfucker." The vampire pulled her in front of him like a coward, using her as a shield, and Devon immediately lost any respect she may have had for him as a legitimate adversary. Wrapping a hand in her hair, he yanked her head violently to the side. Tears filled her eyes again.

The dragon wavered in front of her as it watched them, following the vampire's movements with sharp eyes. Stretching its head forward, it opened its mouth and screeched in anger. Or hunger. It was hard to tell.

Devon cried out as a razor sharp fang tore into her throat. Blood, warm and wet, ran over her collarbone to cool and congeal in the fibers of her sweater. An ingrained survival instinct took over, and she managed to wiggle an arm between them. Shaping her hand into a claw, she found the bulge of soft flesh between the vampire's legs and squeezed as hard as she could, twisting her wrist.

The vampire tore its fang from her throat with a yelp, and Devon was almost as shocked as him that her technique had worked. She took advantage of his surprise by slamming the back of her head into its face. Then she threw her body forward with such force she stumbled forward about five feet before she fell. Scrambling to her feet, she ran toward her car.

The ground shook beneath her feet and a sudden gust of wind blew her hair into her face. She tried to keep her footing, but it was near impossible. Stumbling every few steps, Devon's foot landed in a hole she had no way of seeing and her ankle twisted painfully. With a cry, she fell forward, barely catching herself before she face planted.

She managed to struggle to her feet again, but when she tried to put her weight on her ankle, it gave out. Through strands of wet hair—wet with what, she didn't even want to know—she saw the vampire disappear in the direction of trees. There one moment and gone the next, leaving her on her own with the dragon.

It was right behind her. She felt the warmth of its breath on her damp back. Panic shot a surge of adrenaline into her blood, and she got to her feet. She made it two steps before she fell again. Pulling her good leg beneath her, she pushed with her hands—

And was hit around the midsection and lifted into the air. Wind whooshed past as she watched the ground grow farther and farther away. Pushing her hair out of her face, she found herself directly beneath the dragon's belly. Large wings flapped lazily as it gained altitude.

Devon drew in a ragged breath, and screamed.

She must've startled her rescuer, because her stomach

lurched just like it did in airplanes when they hit air pockets. "Oh...God! Please don't drop me!" she shouted.

The dragon responded by tightening its talons around her middle.

Though her hands were cold and aching, she did her best to hang on. Long minutes passed with Devon taking turns praying to anyone who happened to be listening and trying to convince Kohl not to barbecue her alive, and then her stomach flipped as they plummeted toward the ground. He skimmed the tops of a group of trees until they came to a clearing. There, the dragon tucked in its wings and descended rapidly toward the ground. Rearing up at the last minute, it gently deposited her on the grass between two mounds of cactus.

Devon pushed herself up onto her knees just in time to watch him land like some giant, ancient bird just a few feet away from her. The large head swung from side to side, nostrils flaring as it scented the air. Then he cocked his head to the side, and she got the impression he was listening, though she didn't know how he could hear anything with such tiny ears on top of his head. When he appeared satisfied, his glowing eyes found her. A low purring sound rumbled deep within his throat.

Afraid to move, she tried to gauge his mood. But he seemed perfectly content to stand guard over her for the time being. From this angle, Devon saw more wounds on his neck and shoulder, and one of his wings was torn near the second spike closest to the tip. Slowly, she stood on her good leg and tested her ankle. It was sore, but she could walk on it now.

The dragon—Kohl—speared her with one glowing eye. She stilled, her blood freezing in fear she was about to be flambéed like the soup she'd eaten earlier, but he only huffed as though to fuss at her for trying to walk and went back to surveying the area around them.

It took a few seconds, but eventually her heart gave a couple of good hard pounds and then settled into its natural rhythm again. Devon swallowed hard and looked around, trying to figure out where they were. But the moon was hidden behind the clouds, and it was impossible to see very much at all. It was even darker than it was on the lake. At least there, the houses across the way gave her some point of reference. If it weren't for the dragon's eyes, she wouldn't be able to see anything at all.

Devon turned her attention back to her companion.

As if sensing her attention, he shifted about restlessly, favoring his wounded shoulder. It looked like he was trying to tuck his body in on itself, as though to appear smaller.

She crossed her arms against the cold, intentionally ignoring him. She didn't know what she could do to help him anyway, even if he would allow her to get close enough to look at his injuries.

But it only took a few seconds for her to admit defeat. She wasn't one to stand by and watch creatures suffer, no matter what they were. So, she looked to the heavens for strength, then back at the dragon. "Please don't eat me. Or worse, burn me alive."

The eye facing her slowly closed and opened again as another purr rumbled through him in response.

Careful of her bad ankle, she limped over. When she was close enough, he lifted his injured wing. Devon froze, ready to duck, but he only tucked it around her like a shield.

He was still protecting her.

She took a steadying breath.

"My heart is never going to survive this night, you know that?" She waved her hand in the air as her sanity threatened to snap. "Forget what I said before about wanting to see the dragon. I want Kohl back. Can you do that for me?"

The dragon blinked its eye, and made a clicking sound in the back of its mouth.

"No? Really?" She rubbed her forehead. "Okay, then. Well, at least having a dragon for a boyfriend distracts me from being involved in a mass shooting." Slowly and carefully, she laid one hand against his side. His scaly skin was slightly different than, say, a lizard. Softer. But not as soft as a human's, or a vampire's for that matter. And also unlike a lizard, he was warm.

His side rose and fell beneath her hand as he breathed deep, and she could feel the slow, steady rhythm of his heart. This close, the natural woodsy scent that clung to him was stronger than when he was in his human/vampire form, but still achingly familiar.

She touched the wing, running her fingers as far as she could reach. Strong bones. Smooth, leathery expanse of skin between them marred only by the zigzag of veins. She didn't touch the spikes, not knowing how sharp they were, or if they were venomous or otherwise dangerous, and now wished she'd spent more of her time at Parasupe reading the studies in their database about dragons. Vampires and werewolves had always been more interesting to her, as no dragons had ever been found on this continent. Until now.

Steadying herself with one hand on his body, she limped to his shoulder as he tracked her movements. Lifting up onto her tiptoes with a wince of pain, she tried to check out the wound.

He was so large, though, she couldn't see anything but blood running down his wing.

His large head swung forward, and again, he lifted his nose and scented the air. She wondered if all dragons did that, or if it was because of his vampire side. When he appeared content there was no danger, he lowered himself with a grunt until he was lying on his belly and his shoulder was just above her head.

Carefully, Devon gently probed the area around the wound, but without enough light, it was impossible to see how deep it went. The good news was, the bleeding appeared to be slowing, so either it wasn't very serious, or he healed extremely fast. She wondered what had caused it. It had to have been a weapon of some sort, for surely a vampire alone couldn't rip open a wound this large, but she didn't remember seeing anything.

Of course, she *had* been running for her life.

One hand on the powerful slab of muscle, she made her way down the length of his neck until she reached his head. He didn't lift it from where it rested on the ground, but that striking eye continued to watch her every move as she checked out the wound on his face, easier to see in the glow from his iris. When she saw it wasn't near as bad as the one on his shoulder, she met his stare.

It was at that moment Devon realized Kohl had been wrong. "You know exactly who I am, don't you?"

The dragon purred, the sound content.

She felt strange talking to him like this. "Thank you for saving me." Her ankle began to ache, and she leaned back against his large neck and looked around. "So, are we just going to stay here all night, or...?"

His sides heaved as he took in a deep breath. Readjusting his head and body a bit, he settled into the damp ground.

"I guess so." Suddenly cold and exhausted, she looked around for a good place to sit, and finally decided to just stay right where she was. Luckily, it was winter and she didn't have to worry about fire ants. But on the other hand, it was winter and it was fucking cold.

Careful of her ankle, she sank to the ground and leaned back against the dragon's warm neck. Exhausted, her eyes closed even as she shivered, and Devon felt his wing cover her as she drifted off.

Her last thought was wondering if she was going to wake up to discover this had all been some kind of crazy dream.

CHAPTER 13

Kohl shivered as he gradually became aware of cold rain trickling down his bare back and warm woman snug in his arms. Blinking his eyes open, he instantly realized where they were.

Or, where they *weren't*, was more apt.

Completely alert in an instant, a quick assessment showed there was no immediate danger. Not from the sun, and not from vampires. Like any other predator, he knew instantly if any others of his kind were near. He touched his face and shoulder, feeling the remnants of some pretty serious injuries. Healing from wounds of this caliber took a lot out of him, making shifting back an experience he'd rather not remember, and he usually didn't. He must've passed out. Looking up at the sky, he saw some clouds had rolled in, and it was hard to judge what time it was, but he would guess they had a good three hours before sunrise. Plenty of time for him to get them out of the open.

Devon shivered in his arms as the rain wet her face, and his body hardened instantly, eager to remind him that three hours gave them time to do plenty of other things, also. He resisted the urge to press his hips into the softness of her ass. Barely. But he couldn't stop himself from tightening his hold around her waist and lowering his nose to her fragrant curls.

And then he smelled the blood.

His fangs extended as he carefully rolled her over, scanning her body for injuries.

There was a deep puncture wound in her neck. A wound he knew he hadn't put there. He would remember if he'd fed from her. His blood would recognize her, and there'd be *two* fang punctures.

Kohl stared in utter shock.

Motherfucker.

Something harsh and primitive began churning in his gut, slowly working its way up to the surface. He realized he was making sounds he'd never heard himself make before. Possessive sounds. Violent sounds.

Devon blinked awake, and one hand came up to shield her face from the rain while the other reached for him, landing on the side of his face and jaw. "Kohl? You're back." She smiled in the dark, but it quickly fell from her face. "What's wrong?" She tried to get up, but his arm lay heavy across her middle and he made no effort to release her.

She shivered again from the cold, the movement rubbing her ass provocatively against him. Though he knew she hadn't done it on purpose, the urge to bite her was so strong, it took him a few seconds to answer. "You've been claimed."

Her hand left his face and blindly felt the side of her throat. She probed the wound, and her fingers came away wet with blood. She rubbed the tips together. "He bit me." Her voice had a faraway quality to it, and her emotions were...numb.

But Kohl was far from feeling such a lack of sensation. "He claimed you as his to feed on," he repeated. Disgust and disbelief dripped from his voice. Not toward her. Never at her. No. This was aimed all at himself as the urge to put her fingers in his mouth and suck off the blood that smelled so fucking good, to sink his fangs deep into her throat, nearly overcame any other thought in his head. The instinct was so strong, he very nearly acted on it without thinking. But he caught himself just in time.

He knew who had done this. There was only vampire it could possibly be. Still, he wanted to be sure. The attack earlier was little more than a red haze in his mind. He caught her eyes with his. "Devon, who bit you?"

Anxious eyes searched for and found his. "I don't know. I'd never met him before. He wasn't at the club the other night. Or at least I never saw him."

"What did he look like?"

She frowned. "Um...like a vampire. Black eyes, fangs." He could see her struggling to remember, and tried to be patient. Rushing her wouldn't help anything. "No. He only had one fang. The other one was broken, or removed or something. Light skin. Long, dark hair. Oh! And I think he was wearing a jean vest?"

Something way beyond anger rose within him, temporarily burying the instinct to feed beneath the more immediate need to smash his fist into Jaz's face until he felt bones turn to powder beneath his knuckles, right before he ripped off the bastard's dick and shoved it down his own throat. "Jaz." Kohl closed his eyes, reigning in the violence surging through him.

149

It wasn't like him to feel such rage toward another. Especially not someone like Jaz. He felt the softness of Devon's palm on his cheek, then his jaw, and then the side of his neck.

"I wish I could see better in the dark."

Her sultry voice, tinged with worry, combined with her hand wandering lightly over his shoulder to feel his bare chest, and lower, instantly distracted him and intensified his lust. But not for Jaz's blood.

For her.

He caught her wrist before she found out how much she affected him. Somewhere at the edge of his consciousness he realized the rain had stopped. "Devon, we need to get to shelter before the sun comes up."

"What's wrong? Everything's okay. You didn't hurt me. Why are you so upset?" She pulled her arm from his grip and touched his face. "I can't see very well, but I can feel it. The strain in your expression. The tension in your muscles." Her fingers wandered over his mouth and one finger skimmed his fang. "This. It's just a bite. It'll heal…right?"

It would be easy. It would be so easy. All he had to do was bite down, just a little, and the tip of his fang would pierce her fingertip and he would be able to taste her.

With a moan, he pulled his head back out of her reach. "We need to go." Jaz had her blood in his system. He'll be looking for them, and if they didn't get the fuck out of there, he would find them. And who knows what he'll do in his state of mind? "We need to go, Dev."

"I don't think you mean that."

"You're wrong. I do."

"Then why won't you let me sit up?" She smiled. "Are you embarrassed that I'll see you naked? Because trust me, honey, from what I can tell by looking at you *in* your clothes, you don't have a damn thing to worry about in that department."

With a start, Kohl realized that not only did he have her trapped between his arms as he leaned over her, pressing her down with his weight, but his leg was thrown intimately between hers. He closed his eyes, but he couldn't bring himself to move away. "No. It's not that. I'm a shifter. I'm used to it."

"Then why?"

His voice was barely above a whisper when he painfully admitted, "Because I want it to be me." He pulled air into his lungs, and repeated his confession, louder. "I wanted it to be me."

He heard the rush of her blood with each rapid beat of her heart, so easily discernible to his vampire hearing, and knowing how he affected her only made it worse. The scent of her desire filled his nose, intensifying the lure of her. With a moan, Kohl dropped his forehead to hers.

Her hands tightened on his shoulders. "What does it mean? When you say he claimed me? It's not just that he bit me. Is it?"

He studied her face. Her eyelids were dark, the lids heavy, her lips slightly parted. Her tongue peeked out to wet the bottom one.

"No."

"What does it mean?"

Her damp sweater was warm, heated from their skin. The soft wool grazed his nipples when he shifted closer, sending a shot of lust straight to his groin, scattering his thoughts. It took him a few seconds to compose himself. "He drank from you. Your blood is in his system."

"What does that *mean*, Kohl?"

He tried breathing through his mouth. "It means we need to

get the fuck out of here, before he finds us. If he gets anywhere within a couple of miles of you, your blood will call to him and he'll be able to track you like a hunting dog."

But she was shaking her head before he'd finished his sentence. "You need to fix it. How do we fix it?"

He continued to breathe in and out of his mouth. All it did was make his mouth water. "I can't fix it." Because the only way to fix it was for him to override Jaz's claim with his own, and that wasn't fixing it. That was just transferring the right to her blood from one vampire to another.

"So, I just run? For how long?"

"Just until I can take care of him." And he realized at that moment that he meant every word. He *would* take on Jaz. He would take on the entire coven if it meant keeping Devon safe. He didn't know when it had happened, or how. Maybe that night at the club when the bullets were flying and all he could see was her. Maybe it was before that, when he saw her on the news, so beaten down and fragile and yet so fucking brave. Maybe it was after the attack last night, and the discovery that even the dragon was falling for her. But she was suddenly very precious to him. And he was not willing to give her up so easily.

"What if you took more? What if you bit me and took more? Would you have a higher claim to me or whatever?"

He held back a groan. Why was she doing this to him? "Yes, technically. But…"

"But, what?"

Her asking him to drink from her aroused him to a whole new level.

No. He shook his head. "I can't, Devon. I can't do that." Not without having a conversation about what that would mean.

"Is it against vampire law, or something?"

"Not exactly. It's more an unspoken rule not to move on another vampire's territory, one that could have unpleasant consequences, depending on the situation."

Knowing if they stayed like this any longer his vow to himself would mean nothing, he forced himself to move off of her.

She sat up, too, catching his hand before he could leave her. "But, I want you to do it."

Despite the intense effort it took him to be this close to her and still control himself, especially with the open wound in her throat, he gently pushed a stray curl from her face with a trembling hand. "We need to talk about things before this happens. There's a lot we need to talk about, Devon."

Her jaw clenched. "I don't care about any of that. Not if it's with you."

"Let's say I do this. Let's just say I do. You'll only be free *of Jaz*, the vampire who attacked you." He left the rest of it unspoken. She was a smart woman. She would know what that meant.

Her lips pressed into a thin line. "But it would be you."

God, she was stubborn. He gave up trying to get through to her. He just didn't have it in him right now. "Devon, please."

"Kohl, what will happen if you don't?"

He didn't even want to think about that. But it was simple. "He'll hunt you, because it will be fun for him and because he can. If you try to run, it will only make the game more interesting. He'll be able to find you anywhere."

"And what will happen if he does? What then?"

"Devon..."

"What then, Kohl?"

He rubbed the back of his neck, not missing the way her eyes followed his movements in the dark. "Then he'll either kill you, on purpose or accidentally, or take you back to the coven and do whatever the fuck he wants to you. And no one will stop him."

"Because he claimed me." There was a weighted pause. "Except I'm not his. I'm yours."

Kohl dropped his hand to his thigh. "Fucking hell," he growled.

She reached for him, but seemed to rethink her decision and dropped her arm.

He caught it before it hit the ground. Turning her hand over in his, he brought it to his mouth and softly kissed the center of her palm. He couldn't think straight lying here like this with her. They needed to get the hell out of there. He played with her fingers as he said, "I'm not doing this in the middle of a field."

"Kohl, we don't have time."

But he kissed her hand again. "We have time enough to get you out of the cold. Come with me." Getting to his feet, he pulled her up with him and took her hand. As they started to walk through the damp grass, he glanced back over his shoulder. "And don't be staring at my ass."

Devon burst out laughing, and Kohl couldn't help but smile as he tightened his grip on her fingers and helped her along behind him.

He'd known where he was as soon as he'd woken up. The beast always brought him back to this place, and it was both good and bad. Good because it was a place to land away from seeing eyes, and it was near friends who knew who and what he was. Bad because the damned thing loved to settle down for the night in the middle of an open field. Or worse, sunbathe in that same field if it was still daylight. Kohl had had more than one close call when he'd shifted back while the sun was up, because the dragon loved to bask in the heat of the day. The vampire, however, would burn alive within seconds. It was a cruel twist of nature that had allowed a creation such as him to survive—a male who longed for the warmth of the sun but could only enjoy it in a form he had no memory of.

Just over a slight incline, a little house came into view, and a dim but welcoming light was lit over the back door.

"We're back at the restaurant?"

As they walked into the circle of warmth it cast, Devon tried to catch up to him, and he noticed for the first time she was limping.

Concerned, he looked over his shoulder and caught Devon...looking straight at his ass.

When she noticed he was watching, she averted her eyes and shrugged. "What? You're running around showing it off and you expect me not to look?"

Kohl laughed, and answered her question. "Margaret and her family know what I am. It's safe here."

They got to the door, and he rapped five times. There was some shuffling around inside, and then it was opened by their hostess from earlier. She wore a long nightgown with little pink flowers all over it, her dark hair was braided over one shoulder, and she held a blanket in her hands. She smiled that same welcoming smile and handed him the blanket. "Is everything well?" she asked with her Irish lilt.

He took the blanket from her and wrapped it around his waist. "Devon was bit."

"Not by you, I take it?"

He shook his head.

The smile immediately fell from Margaret's face and she pushed him aside and pulled Devon into the house and under the light. "Oh, no."

Devon complied, allowing the older woman to fuss over her while she looked around the kitchen with interest.

"Who was it?" Margaret asked him.

"It was Jaz."

Her smiling blue eyes narrowed and her mouth hardened. "That fecker. He's not right in the head. He'll be looking for you, you know," she said to Devon.

"She knows," Kohl told her.

"Well, it doesn't look so bad." She patted Devon on the arm with a sympathetic smile.

"Can we stay downstairs?"

"Of course. You don't even have to ask. You know that, Kohl. But I appreciate that you always do." She shooed them in the direction of the restaurant. "Go on, then. You know where to go. There's fresh towels and I can bring some food if you'd like."

"I think we're good, Margaret. Thank you," Kohl told her.

"Speak for yourself," Devon said, turning to Margaret with a hopeful expression. "I'm starving and I lost my leftovers."

Margaret opened the restaurant size refrigerator and pulled out a dish covered in foil. "Just warm it up in the microwave for a minute or two. And let me know if you need anything else, dear," she told Devon. "I'll see you both tonight."

"Thank you," Devon told her.

"Yes, thank you, Margaret. You and your family have saved my ass more times than I would like to admit."

"Well, and a fine arse it is." She gave him a wink, locked the back door, and left through the other side of the kitchen to the rooms she shared with her brother.

"See?" Devon told him. "It's a fine ass."

Kohl's shook his head with a laugh. "I think the loss of blood is starting to affect you. Come on." Leading her in the opposite direction, he took her through the restaurant. There was a door between the two restrooms. He felt along the top of the top of the doorframe and found the key, unlocked it, and turned on the light.

Stairs led down to a basement. It hadn't been an easy task, but with the family's permission, his coven had dug it out years ago for emergencies. Kohl just happened to have more emergencies than the others, so he'd taken to keeping some things of his own there.

Devon preceded him down as he closed and locked the door behind them with the key. When he joined her at the bottom of the stairs, he found her standing in the middle of the floor, looking around in surprise.

"Wow. This place is like something straight out of a James Bond movie."

Kohl tried to see it from her eyes. "Not quite that high tech, but it'll do."

The finished basement had none of the old world charm of the restaurant above. But what it did have was concrete and steel enforced walls, bulletproof doors, a simple but functional kitchen and bath area, and a bedroom with a closet that hid an escape tunnel out the back. No one could get in without the key, and in the case of something happening, any ruckus heard upstairs would give them time to get out through the closet, the escape tunnel would self-destruct, and they wouldn't be able to be followed. "It's safe down here. Jaz won't be able to sense you through these walls. And even if he did, we have a way to get out through the bedroom. But, the sun will be coming up soon. We'll be safe enough for the day."

She turned to him, her face carefully blank. "What about Margaret and her family upstairs?"

Kohl only paused for a brief moment. "They know the risk they take by allowing us to use this place."

Devon stared at him for a minute. There was no accusation in her eyes, but he could feel her judgment. It radiated from her like a blast of cold air. "They know the risk," he insisted. "They chose to do this. As a matter of fact, they offered. We didn't ask. And if anything bad goes down, of course I will do everything within my power to help them." That last part was completely true, but not at the risk of Devon's life.

She nodded and wandered into the kitchen to heat up her food.

He motioned toward the bedroom with his head. "When you finish eating, we'll go take care of your neck."

She obediently nodded.

Kohl poured some red wine, knowing they both could use it, and kept her company while she ate, neither of them saying much. Many times, he felt the heat of her stare on his chest, neck and arms, and he waited for her to ask about his ink. But she never did.

When she was finished, he took her glass and his and left them on the counter. "In the bathroom," he told her.

She found the room, went in, and flicked on the light switch. Faced with her image in the large mirror over the sink, she frowned. Leaning in, she touched the wound. "Good God. That looks deep. I'm glad this doesn't feel as bad as it looks."

"It's a vampire thing. It numbs the pain. Makes our victims

want it so it's easier for us to feed." Pulling her away from the mirror, he turned her around and indicated the side of the tub. "Sit. Please."

She sat.

He'd purposely left the bathroom door open, hoping it would help ventilate the room, but in this small space, the scent of her blood was like a thick fog he couldn't breathe through. Kohl took shallow breaths through his mouth, and saw Devon's eyes flick over his fangs and then down to his bare chest and arms. That so didn't help. "I'm going to try to clean it out as much as I can, okay?"

"Okay."

She sounded nervous. "It might hurt a little bit, Dev. And I'm sorry. But I don't want it getting infected." He was lying. It wouldn't get infected. He just couldn't stand the thought of any of anyone else's DNA lingering inside her. "I'll try to be as careful as I can."

She nodded, watching him with big, brown eyes. But her mouth was set in a determined line, as though she knew what he was about and was in agreement. "Go ahead. Do what you need to do."

He got the supplies he needed from the small closet and wet a cloth with warm water. Kneeling in front of her, he paused just before it touched her skin. He searched her face, hoping she would see he truly meant what he was about to say. "I'm so sorry I let this happen."

A sad smile lifted the corners of her mouth. "I know."

Her sorrow washed over him, heightening his own. Carefully, he washed around the outside of the wound, but she didn't so much as flinch, even when he knew it had to hurt.

"Does it hurt?" she asked.

Lost in thought about what to do about Jaz, he glanced up at her face, but she was studying the wall above the toilet. "Does what hurt?"

"When you shift into the dragon."

Ah. That. "Yeah. It hurts."

Real concern creased her brow as she turned her head to look at him. "I'm sorry."

Taking her chin in his hand, he turned her face away again and continued washing the vampire bite. "I'm used to it."

She was quiet for a few seconds. "What does your tattoo mean? Unscarred."

He rinsed out the cloth. "It means I don't let anything stick to me."

"You don't let things hurt you, you mean."

"It hurts. I just don't let it fuck with me. I don't let it change me." Holding the wound open with the fingers of his other hand, he forced some of the cloth inside.

Her breath hissed between her teeth, but she was tough and didn't pull away. "Everything changes you," she said. "Everything you experience makes you who you are."

It started bleeding again, which was good. The flow of blood would help clean it out. Though his hands shook, Kohl cleaned it out as best he could, then pressed a clean gauze pad against it. By this time he was barely breathing at all.

"The angel on the side of your neck?" Her words seemed to come from far away.

"My mom. And purple roses were her favorite kind."

Still staring at the wall, she asked, "What's the thing in the middle? Between the roses?"

Through a red haze of blood lust, Kohl answered her. "A Harley engine."

"So, you really like bikes, huh?"

He could barely concentrate on her words. "Yeah." He took her hand and pressed it against the gauze until she held it there on her own, then he sat back on his heels.

Her eyes met his, traveled over his face and torso, and returned. He could only imagine what she was seeing. "Sorry about this," she told him.

"It's not your fault." He took a shallow breath through his mouth.

"Is it all cleaned out?"

Kohl nodded. "Think so."

"Good." Tilting her head away, she pulled the gauze away and presented him her throat.

Overwhelmed with what she was offering him, Kohl found he couldn't move.

When she noticed, Devon placed her hands on his shoulders and forced him to look at her. "I trust you, Kohl. Completely."

Ah, honey. You really shouldn't do that.

CHAPTER 14

Devon hoped her words had gotten through to him as she tilted her head away again, exposing her throat to Kohl. A brief second of panic overtook her when she realized what she was about to do, but she pushed it firmly away. She knew from working at Parasupe how enamored victims became of the vampires who bit them. But she didn't know the vampire could track them. And from Kohl's reaction, there were other things she didn't know, but they didn't have time for a big heart to heart. Besides, it all boiled down to one thing —Kohl was a stand up guy for a vampire/dragon, and she would much rather be attached to him than the crazy bastard who'd bitten her, if that was the case.

The first touch was soft, warm…gentle. A reverent kiss she felt all the way to her soul. The second touch was just a taste, a stroke of his tongue followed by a moan so earthy and erotic she felt it all the way between her legs. There was another gentle tug on her skin as he tested the blood flow.

Devon loved being this close to him. She moaned, and felt

Kohl's response as he drank from her. Experiencing this with him was the most intimate thing she'd ever experienced. The earthy, masculine smell of him. The warmth of his skin beneath her hands. The retrained power of his quivering muscles. The helpless sounds he made. Not to mention the knowledge that he needed her to survive—quite literally. No heart to heart or hot and heavy sexual encounter had ever come close to it.

As a woman, she'd always been aware of the effect she had over men, no matter what they preferred to believe. When it came to sex, she held the power. But this...

This was heady in way she'd never imagined possible.

Without leaving her throat, he leaned back until he sat on his heels and pulled her with him, arranging her on his lap. Devon straddled his hips with his strong arms wrapped around her and his hard, hot length nestled between her legs. Her leggings and the thin blanket he wore like a towel provided few barriers between them, but it was still too much as far as she was concerned. Rolling her hips, she tried to feel more of him.

Kohl lifted his head from her throat, dropped his hands to her thighs, and pressed his forehead against hers. "Devon." Her name tore from his lips as his large body shuddered beneath her. "I want more. I want so much more." Then he pulled back to look at her, and the words she had been about to say caught in her throat as she saw him. Really saw him.

Kohl was more vampire at this moment than she'd ever seen him before. His upper lip lifted in a predator's snarl, exposing his long fangs as he studied the pulse in her throat with hungry eyes. His cheekbones were so sharp, she was surprised they didn't cut through the skin. His eyes were bright, glowing that reddish gold, the pupils so narrow they were like slits. And overlaying shadows of the dragon rippled underneath.

Her eyes dropped to his bare chest and shoulders, where muscle strained, giving his tattoos a life of their own. Unable to resist, she ran her hands down the front of his shoulders, over his pecs, and down the hard ridges of this stomach, feeling the skin and muscle ripple beneath her fingertips. His big body shuddered beneath her touch, but otherwise he remained still, allowing her to explore him.

He was scary and miraculous and hungry and…beautiful.

Without a word, she pulled her hair away from the side of her neck and offered it to him once more.

Kohl immediately tried to draw back, turning his face away. He shook his head once, hard. "No. I've taken enough. It's enough." Shame reddened his features and darkened his eyes as he glanced at her sideways. "I already took more than I needed to."

But Devon wasn't giving up that easily. She took his face between her hands, ignoring his hiss of warning, and forced him to look at her. "I want more, too. Kohl, I want so much more with you."

Desperation colored his words. "We can't, honey. I'm barely hanging on by a thread, now."

With a deep breath for courage, she pressed a kiss to the corner of his mouth, the fine hairs of his beard and mustache soft against her lips. "I want to try."

"Devon—"

She could hear the raw need in his voice. He wanted her. And she wanted him. But more importantly, she trusted him.

Even if he didn't trust himself. "You won't hurt me," she told him with conviction.

"You don't know that. What if I shift?"

But his hands were already working their way beneath her sweater. When they came in contact with her heated skin, his eyes closed on a moan.

"You won't." And at that moment, she'd never been more certain of anything in her life.

He wasn't so easily convinced. "How do you know that? I don't know that."

"I just know. Kohl, the dragon is a part of you. You may not remember much when you shift, but he—you—you were gentle, and protective. You saved me. You won't hurt me. You won't shift." Grabbing the bottom of her damp sweater, she pulled it up and off, tossing it to the floor. Then she took his hands and placed them on her breasts. His palms were hot through the thin cotton of her bra. He ran the pads of his thumbs over her nipples, and they strained toward him.

"Kohl, please. I want you to touch me. I want to be with you. I want you inside of me. I want everything with you." She braced for his rejection, knowing it would shatter her when it came. But she needed him to know how she felt. She didn't want him to have any guilty feelings about what was happening.

His chest rose and fell with quick, hard breaths. He glanced up at her once, then slid his fingers beneath the top of her bra on either side.

With a quick, hard tug, he ripped it in half, exposing her bare breasts to his hungry gaze. He stared for so long, her face began to burn. But then one trembling hand covered her breast and squeezed, hefting its weight in his palm.

Eyes filled with wonder rose to meet hers, and Devon gave him a tremulous smile.

She nearly cried out with yearning when he wrapped his other hand around the back of her neck and brought her mouth to his. His kiss was strained, and Devon knew he was holding back. She broke it off to say something, anything that would make him let go, but her thoughts scattered as he kissed his way down to her throat, hovering over the wound he'd fed from.

"Do it," she hissed.

Kohl struck, sharp fangs piercing easily through her skin. Devon did cry out this time, not from pain, but with relief, holding him to her when he would've stopped. "No! Drink, Kohl. Drink from me."

The little bit of discomfort there was vanished almost instantly, replaced by the primal feel of him pulling on her vein. Pleasure shot through her, intensified by his moans and the friction of her nipples against his chest. Still wearing her leggings, she moved her hips, rubbing herself shamelessly against him as waves of desire rolled through her womb, cresting higher and higher, the pressure building with each drink he took and every roll of her hips until—with a ragged intake of breath—she crashed over the edge.

His arms tightened around her as she came, the pleasure too much for her to contain, holding her as still as he could while he greedily partook of the blood rushing through her veins. As she drifted back to reality, he withdrew his fangs from her throat, licking her wounds closed. He kissed his way across her jaw, taking her mouth with an intensity he never had before. He tasted like dark wine and darker desire, and Devon thrilled to the feeling of being truly possessed.

Before she realized what he was doing—he could move so damn fast—she found herself off his lap and on her feet. With her hands on Kohl's shoulders, she braced herself as he removed her shoes and leggings, crying out when his tongue and teeth found her. His fingers dug into her hips, holding her still as he thrust with his tongue, drinking her release with moans of pleasure until the tension built into a furious storm and she crashed around him again, his hands the only things keeping her upright.

Air rushed past, cooling her heated skin, and she opened her eyes to find herself in the bedroom.

Kohl laid her down on top of the simple, blue bedspread. But instead of joining her, he stood staring down at her in all of his naked glory, the blanket left behind somewhere.

Devon took the opportunity to admire his body, large and muscular, and vibrating with power. Tattoos covered his neck, upper chest, arms and hands. Only his "unscarred" mantra marred his stomach. Her eyes dropped lower, down to his hips and his thick, swollen cock, and a new surge of lust had her rubbing her thighs together helplessly.

A sound of desperation rumbled in his chest and he took himself in his hand, lazily sliding up and down his length. Devon's hand drifted between her legs as she watched him pleasure himself. When she couldn't stand it any longer, she tore her eyes away. In his expression, she saw the vampire. But in his eyes, the dragon watched her with a lazy hunger. It didn't frighten her. It excited her.

"I can hear your blood calling to me," he told her. His voice was rough, his words thick on his tongue. "That's never happened before." Lifting one knee onto the bed, he hesitated, then carefully laid his palm flat on her collarbone before letting it drift lazily down between her breasts.

Devon arched her back, desperate for more of his touch.

"I feel the dragon, Dev. He hears it, too. I don't know what it's going to do." His startled eyes flicked up to hers. "I don't think I can do this. I couldn't live with myself if..." He stumbled to a halt, unable to finish.

She didn't know what else to say to convince him his fears were unfounded. "You won't hurt me, Kohl. And I'm done talking about this." She rose to her knees, took his face in her hands, and kissed him, not holding anything back.

Kohl moaned and returned her kiss, careful of his fangs, until she could barely catch her breath. Just as determined to have him as he was to keep her safe, she reached between them and wrapped her hand around him.

His hips jerked forward and he broke off the kiss.

A surge of satisfaction went through Devon. The dragon was wide-awake now.

With a helpless groan, he pressed her back onto the bed. But at the last minute, he rolled so she was on top. "Just in case," he whispered.

He was all hard male and barely restrained power beneath her. She kissed his throat, his beard tickling her nose, then moved down his chest, running her tongue over his nipples before moving down his hard abs. She ran her lips and tongue over every letter of his tattoo, then crawled lower still.

Kohl stopped breathing all together.

As she took him into her mouth, she opened her eyes to find him watching her with a feral hunger burning in his eyes. His fingers twisted into her hair, pushing it back off her face so he could see.

"Holy fuck." The words ended on a groan as she pulled him as far into her mouth as she could, and his head fell back against the pillow. He bent his knees and started thrusting with his hips, his entire body shuddering with need as he gasped her name.

The knowledge that she had a male as dangerous as Kohl completely at her mercy did things to Devon. Wonderful things. Dirty things. She couldn't remember ever having been so turned on before by making someone else feel good.

"Devon, please. I want to be inside you. I *need* to be inside you."

She actually whimpered. Hell, yes. She needed that, too. So she didn't argue when he grasped her around her ribcage and dragged her up his body until she was poised perfectly above him. With her hands on his hard abs, she pulled her knees up to either side of his hips, gasping when he hit that little bundle of nerves.

He found and entered her with one powerful thrust. Devon cried out this time, her head falling back as she arched her body to better accommodate his size. Fully inside, he paused, breathing hard, staring up at her with that same wondrous look before the predator returned. Baring his fangs, he lifted her and thrust again.

She rocked her hips, catching his rhythm, her pulse pounding in her ears as the tension built once more in her womb. She was almost there when Kohl suddenly sat up and sank his fangs into her breast with a possessive growl. Devon came instantly and violently, her cries mixing with his sounds of pleasure as he joined her. When he finished, he licked lazily at the wound he'd made, kissed her other breast, then hugged her to him.

When Devon could breathe again and the world came back into focus, she lifted her head from where it rested on his chest and smiled. "See? I told you he liked me."

Kohl's answering smile reached all the way up to his eyes, once again sweet and nearly back to his normal brown. He pushed her hair back from her face. "Are you all right?"

She kissed him hard on the mouth. "Yes. I'm absolutely wonderful."

"Thank God." He hugged her again, then lay back on the bed, leaving her straddling his hips. "Good." His fingers grazed her nipples, then her stomach, and she realized he was avoiding her eyes. A twinge of panic filled her until he said, "I was terrified, Dev. The entire time." His eyes followed the trail of his fingertips as he traced the bite on her breast. "But my God, I've never had anything like you."

She wondered if he was talking about the blood or the sex. "Can you still hear it? My blood?"

His eyes lifted to hers. "Yes. Like hearing my own heartbeat."

A ripple of unease ran through her. A thread of uncertainty. She'd wanted to have sex with him. More than that. She'd felt the same need to claim him as he claimed to feel for her. She didn't and wouldn't ever regret that decision. But, she could have asked him not to feed any more from her. He would've obeyed her wishes. She was as certain of that fact as she was that she had been born on a Tuesday. However, she'd gotten caught up in the moment and had acted on impulse. She'd wanted to know what it would feel like to have him at her throat, fangs embedded deep. Well, now she knew. It was intimate and exciting and she'd never in her life experienced anything like it.

She just hoped she wouldn't regret it.

He sat up again. "What is it? What's wrong?" Cupping her face, he ran his thumb over her cheekbone. "Dev?"

She gave him a smile. "I just need a shower. And some sleep. A wet field isn't the most comfortable place I've ever spent the night."

"Sure," he told her after a pause, and she knew she wasn't fooling him. But he didn't pursue it. "I think there's even some extra clothes that will fit you good enough to sleep in if you'd like, though I prefer you just like this," he teased. "Come on."

Kohl made love to her again in the shower, holding her tight, like he was afraid she would disappear.

But he didn't bite her again.

CHAPTER 15

In the corner of the room, Kohl watched Devon sleep from his spot on the floor and tried to calm his chaotic thoughts. Nearly impossible with the pulse of her blood singing with every beat of his heart. Not as strong as it was a few hours ago, but still there. All he could think about was the taste of her, the insane surge of strength and energy as her energy force invaded his body, flooding and expanding his cells until he felt he was about to bust out of his own skin.

Yet, even as it caused so much chaos with his vampire side, it had calmed the dragon. The beast had been there the entire time he'd made love to Devon, aware and watching, taking part while still contained. There had been three in the bed. Not two. A constant struggle inside of him between vampire and dragon. Kohl had managed to keep the beast in its lair, but barely.

Until the first sip of her blood.

Kohl didn't understand it, and he had no one to ask, because he was the only one of his kind he was aware of. But feeding from her had somehow calmed the beast, satiating its lust until it was happy to let Kohl take the reins.

But it had still been there, hovering on the edge, aware of everything that had happened. It had enjoyed Devon's hands and mouth and body just as Kohl had, and when he came the dragon roared with its own release.

With a sigh, Kohl pushed aside his anxious feelings and glanced upward. The sun was setting. Soon, it would be time for them to leave here, and he still hadn't decided what he was going to do about Jaz. But at least he'd have no claim to Devon now. Any vampire would clearly be able to scent that she was Kohl's. He had made sure of that. Kohl had no idea what had set him off, but luckily, Jaz's bite had been quick. From the look of the wound and from what she'd told him, Jaz hadn't had enough time to drink much. She could leave, go somewhere far away. At least until all of this mess with Jaz was over. If it had just been a case of Jaz following him out of curiosity, Kohl wouldn't have this sinking feeling in the pit of his stomach. But he hadn't acted alone. Three other vampires had been there with him, all dead now, and there was no way in hell they'd followed Jaz out there. One of the others had to have been in charge, and Jaz, follower that he was, had just gotten roped into it. The one thing Kohl didn't know, was why they'd come after him and Devon at all?

He inhaled deeply, and Devon's sweet scent filled him, calming the fire in his blood. In any case, she was safe enough for now. The only thing that would strengthen their bond was if Devon drank from him, but he didn't want her to do that.

Kohl nearly laughed out loud at that complete and utter lie. He wanted nothing more than to feel her drink from him. But if he allowed that, she would be bonded to him. And if that happened, he would never let her go. She would never be free again.

As though she knew she filled his thoughts, Devon moved restlessly on the bed, turning her head away and exposing the faint discoloration where he'd bitten her. It would heal completely soon, probably within the next twenty-four hours.

He knew from hearing the others talk she would always be a lure for him now, even worse than she was before. It wouldn't hurt him to feed from others, but he would always prefer her.

Kohl rubbed the back of his neck. As if that weren't already the case. He shouldn't have fed from her without discussing this first. Despite her protests and her previous employment with Parasupe, she'd already proven she didn't know all there was to know about his kind. If he'd reduced Devon to some pathetic excuse for a woman by claiming her blood as his own, he would never forgive himself.

He scrubbed his face with his hands. There was nothing he could do about it now. It was too late. He'd just have to deal with his cravings for her until they subsided, or until this mess with Jaz was handled. Then she could make the decision of whether or not she wanted to ever see him again.

In the meantime, he needed to take make sure he was still alive to watch over her and give her that choice. It was time to face the truth. And the truth was that Kohl didn't need to ask who had sent Jaz to go after Devon. There was only one vampire Jaz really listened to—the Master. And the Master had a soft spot for Jaz and tried to make him feel useful whenever the opportunity arose. Maybe he got tired of waiting. Also, the coven leader wasn't particularly caring about the life of a human woman who may or may not expose them to the world, and the others wouldn't dare to say a word against the leader. So, there would be no safe haven for Kohl within the coven if things went bad.

And now Jaz knew the truth about his relationship with Devon. The question was, what was he going to do with this new knowledge?

Kohl didn't want to do it, but it was time to head back to the club and see what was going on. First, however, he would make sure Devon got somewhere safe. Rising from the floor, he went over to the small dresser and found the extra clothes he kept there. He even had extra boots in the closet. He slipped into a pair of jeans and a plain black T-shirt, then he retrieved Devon's sweater and leggings and laid them at the foot of the bed. They weren't the cleanest, but they were dry now and would be warm.

He hated that he had to wake her, but they needed to move. Jaz, like all of the other coven members, knew where this place was and would eventually come looking for them here if he didn't return to the club, and he wanted to uphold his promise when he'd said he would do everything he could to protect the family upstairs. "Dev."

She breathed in deep and rolled over onto her side, facing him.

He kissed her on the temple. "Hey, honey. We need to go."

With a moan of protest, she opened one sleepy eye. "Go where?" Her voice was husky with sleep, and he wished he could crawl into bed and wrap himself around her until he couldn't stand not being inside of her. "I need to get you somewhere safe, and then go back to The Caves."

She pushed herself into a sitting position, blinking against the light he'd left on in the bathroom when he'd gotten up.

"Why are you going back there? What about the dick who bit me?"

An apt description of his feelings toward Jaz right now if he'd ever heard one. "I need to find out what's happening. I lost my phone back at the lake. "

"Isn't there one here you can use?"

"There is, but it's better to do this in person."

She swung her legs around and sat on the edge of the bed, her tawny skin smooth and warm in the glow of the light, and her hair an adorable crazy mess. "Why can't you just stay with me?"

He sat beside her and took her hand. "Dev, we need to talk about everything that happened with us today."

She bit down on her lip and shook her head slightly. She wouldn't look at him.

"What are you thinking?" As ever, he wished he could delve into her thoughts and see for himself.

She didn't say anything for a long time, and when she did, it wasn't what he had expected. "I'm thinking I'm hungry," she said. "Is there any more food in this place?" Giving his hand a quick squeeze, she got up and started getting dressed.

Kohl watched her, memorizing every curve, every mannerism. He had the horrible feeling this might bet he last time he would be so honored. "Devon, we need to talk about this."

But she shook her head. "No, we don't. Not right now." She came around to stand in front of him. "I still want you to come with me. And it's not some crazy vampire victim talk. I'm no victim, Kohl. What I am is a woman who cares about you, and I want you to be safe."

He lifted his head. "You don't need to worry about me, Devon." He tried to hold back a smile as he said this next part, but it didn't quite work. "If anyone tries anything, I'll just huff and puff and burn their house down."

She cocked her head and gave him a look his mother would be proud of.

"Seriously," he told her. "You don't need to worry about me, honey. I'm tight."

She sighed. "All right. Fine. If you promise to call me before dawn." She held up her hands. "Not to check up on you; just so I know you're okay." Grabbing a small notepad and pen from the top of the nightstand, she scribbled a phone number down and gave it to him. "Here. This is Frank's cell."

He took the paper from her and gave her a lopsided grin. "You can check up on me anytime you'd like."

"Kohl."

With a laugh, he promised he would call. "I'll make it a point. If I have to, I'll use Hawke's phone. Although, it might be a text so no one will overhear. Now let's go get your car."

Once they'd fetched Devon's car and he'd deposited her back at her apartment, with a promise her "BFF and neighbor" would keep an eye on her and she wouldn't open her door to *anyone*, even if they appeared human, he made his way back to the club on foot.

At best, he'd expected the Master to be waiting for him, or at least Hawke and a few others to be there to escort him down into the throne room. At worst, he'd expected to walk into his own assassination. But what he didn't expect to find was business as usual.

The club was hopping when he walked in the back door. As he rounded the bar, Andrew came up from grabbing a bottle that was stashed underneath and shot him a grin. "Hey, man! Where've you been?"

It wasn't his night to work, so he accepted the beer Andrew slid down to him and settled in on a barstool to find out what he could. "I, uh, lost track of time. Had to spend the night elsewhere." Not really a lie. Andrew could search his thoughts and find out where he'd really been—and with whom—but he just nodded knowingly and turned to wait on a human customer. There was a band at the club tonight, a way to draw in fresh blood. Kohl tipped his beer up to his mouth, watching the dude beside him head banging along to the song. The guy had long, stringy, black hair, a T-shirt with the band's recent album on the front and "Y'all motherfucking need Satan" scrawled across the back. Kohl's eyes drifted down to the white go-go boots on his feet, and he lifted one eyebrow. Looking around, he saw most of the crowd was dressed in a similar fashion.

Whatever floats their boat, I guess.

He turned back to Andrew and pointed over his shoulder with his thumb at the guy making his way back to the front of the stage. "Is that still a thing?"

Andrew looked at the stage and laughed. "Apparently!"

"I thought that look went out in the 90's."

"Nope. Hair bands are dying off, but cover bands are taking their place, and these old fuckers are still head bangin'."

"Yeah, but what's with the boots?"

"That's something I don't have an answer for." Andrew walked down to the other end of the bar to get drinks for a couple who were both grey-haired and leathery from too much sun and not enough sunscreen, but were still rockin' their sixties biker gear.

Kohl watched Andrew work for a while, biding his time and trying to give the impression all was normal. "Who's helping you tonight?"

"One of the young ones. She just ran out for a break." He looked pointedly at the front entrance, meaning she'd found herself a meal for the night.

"Ah." Taking a swig of his beer, Kohl asked, "Have you seen Hawke?"

"Yeah. Right before I came up. He was talking to a few of the guys about making a supply run or something."

"Or something?"

Andrew popped the cap off a bottle and handed it to a customer, then slid the money he'd left off the bar and rang it up. "We just stocked up on liquor so I'm not sure what we need to make a run for."

Anxiety crept up Kohl's spine like tiny fingers. "Have you seen Jaz?"

Andrew shook his head. "Not tonight. He never came home this morning, either."

Kohl rubbed the back of his neck, then downed the rest of his beer and with a nod at Andrew, headed down to the caverns to find Hawke.

He found him in the throne room with a few of the other guys, talking to the Master. When Kohl wandered in, he was immediately waved over.

As Kohl kneeled in greeting, the Master asked, "What did you find out from the woman, Kohl?" Not one to waste time, their leader always got right to the point.

Rising to his full height, Kohl just stared at him for a moment, not sure what to make of the question. But then he figured he'd play along, and see where things went with it. "She doesn't know anything. Nothing more than what I've already told you. I wined her, dined her, plied her with alcohol. Hell, I even fucked her. She told me lots of stuff, but nothing we didn't already know." Talking about Devon in such a way left a bitter taste in his mouth, but showing he cared would only put more of a target on her back. "She's no threat to us."

"But she's no use to us, either," the Master pointed out. His black eyes held steady on Kohl's.

"Her memories were erased." No one needed to know otherwise. "If she makes you uncomfortable, I can convince her to live somewhere else, or Hawke can." He glanced over at his friend, trying to get feel for what they'd been talking about before he'd come in, but Hawke refused to look at him.

The Master sat back in his seat and chewed the inside of his cheek as he made a show of thinking things over. Lifting his head, he frowned. "Have you seen Jaz, by chance?"

He knew this game the Master was playing. He'd watched him do it too many times to count over the years. Pure force of will kept his heartbeat slow and steady. He knew damn well he'd already talked to Jaz. How else would he have known he'd seen Devon? Any show of guilt at this point would mean an immediate attempt at his life. "No, I haven't." He was tempted to explain more, to babble on as he tended to do when he was nervous, but he refrained.

"Hmph." Rubbing his chin with one hand, the Master stared off into the distance. "Funny. He said he ran into you last night before he disappeared."

"He did. I saw him as I was on my way out."

"But you just said you haven't seen him."

"I haven't. Not tonight. I only just got back myself."

The Master locked eyes with Hawke, and Kohl soon felt his friend probing in his head. He rolled his eyes, playing the game for all he was worth. "Master, I'm not hiding anything from you. And you know Hawke can't read me."

A smirk turned up the corners of his mouth but didn't reach his eyes. "Guess I'm going to have to take your word for it." He waved a hand, as though shooing away the bad vibes in the air. "In any case, it appears the human is no use to us. Take care of her."

Take care of her.

He wanted him to kill her. "Master, as I've said, she poses no threat…"

The Master leaned forward, bringing him eye to eye with Kohl from his raised dais. "Is there something else you need to tell me, Kohl?"

Fuck.

Fuck, fuck, fuck!

Steady. Hold it together. "No. Not a thing."

The Master sat back. "Good. Go help Andrew upstairs. I heard Shelby disappeared to eat a human."

With a nod, Kohl turned on his heel and went to his rooms to change. Devon was safe for tonight. The Master wouldn't expect him to do anything until the bar was closed. However, *he* was in deep shit. The Master had never used that tone with Kohl before when asking him to help out. Without so many words, he was testing him. Testing Kohl's loyalty to him.

Well, let him test it. The good thing was, he appeared to have given up on Jaz and was leaving Devon's fate up to Kohl. Now he just had to figure out how the fuck to fake her death and take the target off her back.

CHAPTER 16

"Dev, where the hell are we going?" Frank pulled up the collar on his coat as he waited for her to unlock the passenger side door.

"You don't have to come," she told him for the fourth time as they got into the car. "Actually, I'd rather you didn't."

"I thought you loved me."

She cranked the engine and got the heater going. Typical of Texas weather this time of year, the temperature had dropped in the hour since Kohl brought her and her car back home. And it was only supposed to get colder. "I do. That's why you shouldn't come with me."

"Well, that ain't gonna happen. According to tall, dark, and scary, I'm supposed to stay with you at all times until he lets me know otherwise." He held up his cell phone. "And call the emergency number for the club you programmed into my phone if I so much as see someone look at you funny."

Devon rolled her eyes. "You've never even met him. How do you know he's tall? Or dark?"

"Because all vampires are tall, dark, and scary. All real vampires, anyway. Otherwise, why even bother?"

"He's not scary."

"Oh, honey. He's scary. Trust me. You probably just haven't seen that side of him, yet."

Oh, honey. If you only knew...

After Kohl had deposited her back at her apartment with Frank, she'd filled him in on everything that happened the night before. Well, not exactly everything, but everything he needed to know. Once he'd gotten over his initial pissyness at being left out of the loop for so long, and the fact that he "no-way no-how" believed nothing had happened between her and Kohl (*I always give you details...you're holding out on me*), he'd stuck to her like a bur and announced he was calling in sick to work until this had all settled down.

Devon did eventually convince him to go home and crash for a few hours, keeping his phone with her and promising she'd wake him first thing in the morning. But, sleep had eluded her as she'd paced from one end of her apartment to the other, worrying her lower lip, and checking Frank's cell every thirty seconds to make sure it was on.

She must've eventually dropped off, though, because the next thing she remembered was waking up on the couch with a foggy head, still wearing the clothes from the night before.

Once she'd showered, Devon took a cue from Frank and called in sick to her employer at the pottery shop. The deliveries she did on the side were on her own schedule. It hit her that tomorrow was only Monday. While Frank got his seatbelt on, she said, "I've only known him for four days, Frank. *Four* days. And look at me. Look at all that's happened."

Frank turned the heater down. "That's a whirlwind love affair if I ever heard one." Then he smiled. "But it's so romantic."

"Ha! Crazy, maybe. But not romantic." Throwing the car into reverse, she backed out of her parking spot. "One thing is for sure. I'm no damsel in distress, and I'm not waiting around for some man to save me. I can save myself, and him, too."

When they arrived at the library, she gave her friend one last chance to back out. "Seriously, Frank. If this goes bad, you'll be seen as an accomplice."

He didn't deign to respond as he got out of the car and waited for her on the sidewalk with his hands in his coat pockets and an obstinate look on his face.

Shaking her head, she shut off the engine and got out.

Inside, Devon was relieved to see plenty of computers available for online use. She had a library card for the few times she needed to get online, but she didn't plan on using it. Taking off her coat, she grabbed the last spot at the very end of the table and hung it over the back of the chair. She had one hour before the library closed for the night.

Frank took up residence beside her. "What exactly are you doing?"

She gave him a look, reminding him to keep his voice down. "Remember what I found in Parasupe's database? The reason I was called into court and my boss went to jail?"

"Yeah. You found out they were killing…" He glanced around. "Supernatural creatures for sport. Basically."

Devon started typing, easily overriding the library's security measures and getting online. "Right. And how much you wanna bet it's still happening?"

"I don't understand. You're going to put your boyfriend on the list?"

She didn't pause what she was doing as she filled him in on the genius plan that had come to her while she was changing clothes. "No. I'm putting the vampire who attacked me last night on that list."

"What? How?"

Devon shot him a warning look, glancing around to make sure no one had noticed his outburst.

Putting one elbow casually on the desk and resting the side of his head in his hand, he lowered his voice. "How the hell are you going to do that?"

"I'm hacking into their system, Frank. And I'm almost there." Her fingers moved swiftly over the keys as she got past Parasupe's first wall of defense. "Almost there," she murmured. The company had either been too stupid or too egotistical to change up their security after chasing Devon out of her chosen career and her home, the security system *she* had put in place. Though, at least they'd changed their passwords. "Annnnd, I'm in!"

"This has got to be against the law in so many ways," Frank groaned.

"Only if you get caught. And I won't get caught." She looked through what she had found. She was deep in the database now. Suddenly, she stopped typing and turned to grin at Frank. "Guess what I just found."

"Well, just hurry up and do it so we can get the hell out of here. I can't believe I let you talk me into this."

Her mouth fell open. "Talked you into it?"

"Just get on with it, Dev." Waving a hand at the keyboard beneath her fingers, he glanced around again.

He was right. There was no time for this. She entered in all of the information, including the general location of the coven. As far as she could tell, Parasupe wasn't aware of the vampire's hideout, or about the club. She wished she could be around to see her old boss's face when they discovered the den of a large vampire coven was right under their noses the entire time.

Her finger hovered over the key. If she pressed it, she would be giving away the location of the coven. If she didn't, Kohl could very well be dead by morning.

"What are you waiting for?" Frank frowned at her.

That was a great question. Her finger lowered another fraction of an inch closer to the key, but the execution was cut short as a sharp pain shot through her temples, blurring her vision.

"Dev. Come on. Do it or don't do it. My nerves can't take much more of this."

Squinting through the discomfort, she hit the key. The pain instantly cleared. "Annnnd....done." She backed out of Parasupe's system, and then the library's. "Let's go." When Kohl texted her, she would tell him to get out of there, and take anyone he cared about with him.

"Should we get a book? Make it look like we were here for a real reason?"

"When's the last time you read a book?" She put on her coat as Frank did the same.

"What? I read."

"You read Fitness magazine. And not for the workout advice."

Frank raised his eyebrows as if to say, "Your point?"

"Let's just go. I come in here and use the computers like this all the time. No one will think anything about it."

"Except you never logged in. And what about cameras?"

"I took care of it. Come on." Waving to the young librarian, she pulled Frank out the front door and back to her car.

"Now what do we do?" he asked once they were inside with the heater running.

"Now, we go home, and we wait."

They drove in silence all the way back to the apartments, but as they pulled into a spot near the door, Frank asked, "Is your vampire coming over tonight?"

Devon shut off the car. "He's not *my* vampire."

"Except that love bite on your neck tells me an entirely different story."

Devon flipped down her sunshade and opened the mirror. Sure enough, her scarf had slipped, revealing two healing puncture wounds. "Dammit." She yanked it back up.

"I knew you weren't telling me everything."

She didn't even have to look at him. She could hear the pout in his voice. "Frank, it's just…" She heaved a sigh. "It's complicated." Opening her door, she got out.

"'It's complicated' is a Facebook status meaning you were stupid enough to fall for your booty call, not a real life relationship status," he said from behind her as they hurried inside out of the cold.

"There is no relationship." Not exactly.

"I find it hard to believe that a guy who goes to such great lengths to protect you is just after a one night stand. Or two."

"It's not that. It's just…"

"It's complicated." Sarcasm dripped from his voice. Rolling his eyes, Frank took her keys from her and opened the door.

"Yeah," she muttered. Then followed him inside.

"What do you think he's going to do when he finds out you just put his entire coven on Parasupe's radar?"

Devon hung up her coat. "What are you talking about?" Her head began to pound. "I'm gonna go lie down."

She left Frank standing at her kitchen counter with a look of puzzlement as she went into her room and shut the door.

CHAPTER 17

"Son of a bitch. Shit. Shit!"

Kohl walked into Hawke's room after his shift at the bar, just in time to see the vampire shove his chair away from the computer monitor on his small desk, sending it crashing into the wall. The rest of the room was sparse, with only a bed and a single chair Hawke liked to read in.

"What's wrong?"

Hawke stood. "Your little girlfriend, that's what's fucking wrong."

"What are you talking about?" He quelled the urge to whip out the new cell phone he'd gotten from the stash in his room and call her. Belatedly, he remembered he was supposed to text her after he got back and let her know he was okay. Shit.

"I'm talking about this." Hawke pointed at the computer monitor.

The screen showed four different pictures, feeds from the security cameras that were rigged in the trees around the club. All four showed teams of Parasupe "prosecutors," fully decked out in combat gear and weapons, sneaking around the perimeter of the club.

It was a raid.

"Fuck." Kohl couldn't believe what he was seeing.

"We gotta get the hell out of here," Hawke said, grabbing his coat off the chair by the bed. "More will be coming."

Kohl pointed at the screen. "This isn't Devon, man. She wouldn't do this."

"Are you sure about that?" Without waiting for an answer, Hawke disappeared to warn the others.

Alarms sounded, echoing within the caverns, and the computer screen went black.

"She wouldn't do this," Kohl whispered.

But no one was around to hear.

THREE HOURS LATER, he knocked on her apartment door. She opened it so fast he wondered if she'd been waiting for him. But that didn't make sense. Why would she still be up this late?

Unless…

Her eyes ran over him from head to toe. "What the hell happened? Why didn't you text me?"

He had the funniest feeling she knew exactly what had gone down at the club, and why he was standing at her door in the middle of the night in clothes that were torn from running through the brush and covered in blood, yet the look of innocence on her face could have won her an academy award.

Not his blood. If he'd been hit by any of the bullets those Parasupe fuckers used, he wouldn't be standing here. "May I come in?"

She stepped back out of the way. "Of course."

Her friend—what was the guy's name?—Frank. Yeah, that was it. Frank was spread out on her sofa in nothing but a pair of red lounge pants eating popcorn and watching some reality show on her television.

"Frank, this is Kohl. Kohl...Frank."

Frank froze, a handful of popcorn halfway to his mouth. He dropped it back in the bowl and whispered loudly to Devon, "You *have* been holding out on me."

If Kohl didn't know for a fact that the guy was way more turned on by him than her, he would've been more concerned about his chosen attire. "Hey, man. Would you give us a minute, please?"

Frank gave him another once over, lingering on the blood staining his white shirt this time. To his credit, Frank took Kohl's appearance in stride. "Hard night at the office?"

"Something like that."

Swinging his legs off the couch, Frank stood and planted a kiss on Devon's cheek. "Yell if you need anything, my love." Giving her a look Kohl couldn't decipher, he set the popcorn bowl on the kitchen counter and let himself out.

"What happened?" she asked as the door closed behind him. "Why didn't you text me?"

Kohl walked over to the window and stared out at the city of Austin, lit up under the clear night sky. For once, he was having a difficult time looking at her. He wished he could pull the answer to his question out of her head. "Dev, what did you do?"

The silence stretched on, and he realized he didn't need to be able to read her mind. The fact that she didn't immediately answer told him everything he needed to know.

"Kohl, please tell me what happened. Are you all right?"

"Why did you do it, Dev? Why did you lie to me?"

"I didn't lie to you about anything."

Her emotions were strangely calm for a woman who was in danger of having her life ended any moment. He wanted to turn around. He wanted to turn around and take her in his arms and carry her into that tiny bedroom and fuck the truth out of her. "You don't seem surprised that I showed up at your door in the middle of the night with blood all over my clothes." Needing to see her face, if for no other reason than to torture himself in the long, lonely nights to come, he turned around.

Devon was standing a few feet behind him, hands twisted in front of her. Her hair was covered in some kind of colorful cloth, accentuating her oval face, not one drop of makeup covering her smooth, tawny skin. She was wearing a loose T-shirt and flannel pajama pants. Her feet were bare. She was beautiful. So beautiful it made his mouth go dry and his dick hard, even now. He inhaled to get his bearings, and her scent flooded his senses. The thirst hit him hard. His fangs descended in anticipation of tasting her sweet blood, but he clamped his jaw together, denying them both.

She dropped her chin, looking down at the floor. When she again looked up at him, there were tears in her eyes. "Are you all right? Please tell me."

He didn't want to believe it. Couldn't believe it. Not until this very moment. "You sent Parasupe after me?" He had a hard time getting the words out.

Confusion crossed her features and she shook her head. "No! Kohl, please. Tell me what happened!"

But she didn't fool him. Not any longer. Hawke had been right. "You sent them. *You* sent them."

Again, she shook her head. "I didn't send anybody. I just—"

She winced and touched her temple with one hand, then took a step toward him. "Dammit, Kohl! You were supposed to text me."

Linking his hands behind his neck, he stared up at the ceiling. The dragon was unusually quiet. Surprising, considering the rollercoaster of emotions freefalling around inside his gut so hard it made him want to throw up. Kohl was both glad and sorry about its timing. Glad because even after knowing what he did, he couldn't bring himself to want to hurt her. Sorry because for the first time in his fucked up life, at this moment, he would welcome the oblivion of shifting.

"Kohl, please. Listen to me."

Dropping his arms back down to his sides, he bared his fangs at her in warning. "I don't think so, Devon."

Her eyes flared their own warning. "Kohl."

Deliberately, he walked around her, heading toward the door.

"Kohl! Where are you going?"

He paused at the door, but didn't turn around. "You need to leave, Devon. Pack your bags and get the hell out of this city. Out of this state. Tonight. Right now. The coven knows it was you. I can't protect you anymore. Not right now. Get the hell out of here until I figure out what to do." He let himself out, closing the door gently behind him. A familiar scent wafted past his nose, but it was there and gone so fast he didn't have time to place it.

When he got back out to his bike, he realized something that he'd been too distracted to notice before.

Her blood call was weaker than before. As a matter of fact, he could barely feel her at all.

Kohl felt no relief that their bond was nearly severed. He

only felt alone. Perhaps it had never really been there to begin with. An ugly laugh rose up from his gut and burst from his lips.

He started the engine and lifted the bike off its kickstand.

Devon came running out of the building. Either it took her a minute to follow him or he hadn't realized how fast he'd wanted to get out of there. She stopped when she saw him across the lot, tears running silently down her cheeks.

Kohl saw a crossroads before him. One road led back to the only family he'd ever known, the ones who had taken him in and protected him when he and his mom had nothing and no one. The other road led him to the woman standing shivering in the cold, tears running down her face, who, despite everything she'd done, was still so full of light it warmed him down to his soul and made the dragon purr with pleasure.

But the light wasn't enough to pierce the darkness of her betrayal.

Shifting the bike into first gear, Kohl rode away from her and headed back to help the others get rid of the evidence of the raid.

The dragon spread its wings and screeched in protest. Kohl bared his fangs back at it and hissed into the wind. Four vampires had died. Four young, innocent vampires who hadn't done anything to anyone. They'd died because they'd tried to run instead of taking shelter down in the safety of the caverns while the elders took out the Parasupe team. It hadn't been hard. The humans in the club never even knew anything unusual had happened other than the fact the vampire working the door who wouldn't let anyone leave until he got the okay from Hawke or the Master—a simple enough task of planting the suggestion in their customer's minds that they weren't ready to go home yet.

They'd been lucky this time, but he knew from what had happened to other covens that they wouldn't get away so easily next time. And there would be a next time, thanks to Devon. Now that Parasupe knew where they were, they'd be back. Especially after the first team didn't come home. Fuck, the entire coven might as well be walking around with giant targets on their backs. Himself, included.

Laying low on his bike, Kohl kicked it into high gear.

Halfway back to the caverns, he came up to the intersection that would lead him to the restaurant where he'd taken Devon. At the last minute, he leaned into a sharp right turn. The back tire spun beneath him on some loose gravel, but he leveled things out and sped west. He needed to warn Margaret and her family. If the coven turned on Kohl after hearing what happened the night before, it could very well spill over onto the family. They all knew how close Kohl was with them, and with a vampire's vindictiveness, would go after anyone he cared about just to hurt him.

The image of Devon crying in the cold flickered within the glow of his headlights. With a snarl, Kohl shook his head and the image dispersed. He'd thought he could trust her. He'd been horribly wrong.

He could only hope she'd heed his warning and get the hell out of Austin, because despite what she'd done, he had no wish to see her dead.

CHAPTER 18

Devon threw her suitcase on the bed and started yanking open drawers and stuffing things into it. She had no idea what. She could barely see through the damn tears. She didn't waste time changing out of her pajamas. She'd do that when the sun rose and she could stop somewhere and catch her breath.

It took her a few seconds to realize the incessant pounding she heard wasn't her throbbing head, but the front door.

"Dev? Open up! It's me."

With a sob, Devon kept packing. She couldn't talk to Frank right now. She didn't know why Kohl was so upset with her, but it was obviously some kind of mistake. However, she wouldn't be able to fix it if she was dead.

"Devon, what the hell are you doing? Didn't you hear me knocking?"

She slammed her suitcase shut and zipped it closed. Running to her closet, she got her coat. "How the hell did you get in here, Frank?"

"I used my emergency key."

"That's for emergencies only."

"Well, right now my best friend is running around her room packing every piece of clothing she owns except for essentials—like underwear—and sobbing like someone just died. I'd say that constitutes an emergency."

"I can't right now, Frank. I have to go." Sliding her suitcase off the bed, she pulled up the handle. It took her three tries to get it rolling correctly.

Frank let her pass, following her into the other room and watching her while she found her purse. "When you didn't come get me after I heard your vampire leave, I thought I'd better come check on you. Hey." He grabbed her arm as she passed on her way to the front door. "You don't have any shoes on."

Devon looked down at her bare feet. "Shit." Dropping her stuff on the floor, she ran back into her room. When she came out, sneakers on her feet, Frank was holding her coat and purse. She tried to grab them from him. "I have to go, Frank."

He held it up out of her reach. "And where the hell are you going, Devon? Were you seriously just gonna take off and not say a word to me? What's going on?"

That's exactly what she'd planned to do, because this was too damn hard. Then it hit her. She grabbed his shoulders. "Come with me. You have to come with me."

He raised one eyebrow. "Where, darlin'? Jesus, Dev, you're a mess. You look like you're running from the mob."

"Not the mob. Worse. Vampires."

He dropped his arms back down to his sides. Her purse fell to the floor. "Oh, shit. He knows."

"Knows what?" She could barely concentrate on what he

was saying. Her brain was trying to pound its way out of her skull.

"He knows you sent Parasupe after them, Dev. What the hell else would it be?"

Devon stilled. "What did you say?"

But Frank was pacing now, back and forth, back and forth in front of her. "I told you it was a shitty idea."

"Frank. What the *hell* are you talking about? I didn't send anyone after Kohl or his friends!"

He stopped and looked at her with a worried expression. "Dev, we went to the library. You hacked into their system. You as good as gave them directions to the coven." Suddenly, his face cleared. "Fuck me. You don't remember. You don't remember any of this, do you?"

Devon felt like his fist was wrapped around her heart, squeezing. He was telling the truth. She knew Frank. They trusted each other with their secrets. He'd never lied to her. "Tell me again," she ordered. "Tell me exactly what happened. What was said. Everything."

He did. Every detail. And with every word, she felt like someone was cracking open her skull with a pickaxe.

When he was finished, she sank down onto the arm of her sofa, leaned over, and put her head in her hands and rocked back and forth. "Oh my God."

"You wanna tell me what happened now?"

"Parasupe raided Kohl's coven tonight."

"That would explain the blood."

"And it was my fault."

"Yes, it was."

She looked up at her only friend. "What the hell did I do? He's so angry with me."

One hand on his hip, Frank rubbed away the lines of stress on his forehead. "And you're running because you think he's going to come back and hurt you?"

"No." She shook her head. "Not Kohl. The rest of his coven. They know it was me."

Frank threw his hands in the air. "Dev, what did you think was gonna happen?"

She laughed, but the sound was ugly. "I don't even remember doing it." And now, she not only may have lost any chance at being with Kohl again, but she may have caused his death, along with everyone he cared about. Or worse, Parasupe would find out what he is, and take him back to their labs. And she couldn't even take the time to process how she felt about that, because if Parasupe didn't get to them first, she was about to have a coven of pissed off vampires on her ass. The chances of surviving their wrath was pretty much zero, but she had to try.

Waving her hands back and forth as she tried to breathe, she said, "Someone must have gotten in here." She twisted her fingers together in her lap. "I never should have sent you home to sleep. God, I'm so stupid."

She felt Frank's hand on her hair. "Awe, honey. You're far from stupid. You're just in love."

"I'm not in love. Lust, maybe," she admitted.

"Same thing."

Wiping her eyes, she stood. "I have to go."

"Wouldn't it be better to wait until you hear something?"

She shook her head. She was in some serious shit. "Kohl told me to leave. Right now." She picked up her coat and her purse.

"I'll get my stuff," he said. "Give me one minute."

But she stopped him. "No, Frank. You should stay here. That was just me panicking before. I just…I really don't want to be alone. But you should stay. It's safer here than with me. If the vampires find me they won't stop to ask questions."

"Dev, I really think you should stay here. They can't get in, right? Not without an invitation?"

"No, but—"

"Then I don't understand why you're leaving right now. It's safer here."

"Kohl told me to leave the city. And despite everything, I trust him, Frank." She gave him a quick hug. "I'll call you in the morning when I stop somewhere."

He followed her to the door. "Devon."

"I'll call you." Blowing him a kiss, she checked the hall. As her heart ripped into a million pieces and tears poured down her face, she ran down to her car, suitcase bumping along the stairwell.

CHAPTER 19

Hawke watched the last customer stagger out the front door of the club and into the cab he'd called for him, then checked his cell phone for any word from Kohl. He'd taken off on his bike like a bat out of hell after they'd dealt with those Parasupe fuckers, leaving the others to take care of the evidence, and Hawke wanted to make sure Kohl stayed gone until he could assess the Master's state of mind. Their leader would want someone to blame for this, and Kohl was the obvious answer. Not because anyone would think he'd turned on his own coven, but because he'd allowed the human woman to live long enough to become a threat.

With a nod to Mark at the door, he started to head down to the caverns, but changed his mind and stopped behind the bar to grab a bottle of their best vodka. It wouldn't do much to relax him, but he was feeling the intense urge to drink.

As he poured himself a healthy double shot, he heard voices coming from the hall, and then the soft click of a door closing.

The office door, by the sound of it. Curious, he took his glass with him and with a quick glance around to make sure everyone was gone, walked silently down the hall, stopping just outside the door.

The Master was talking, his voice so low Hawke wouldn't have been able to hear him if he hadn't been standing right outside, even with his vampire hearing.

"I'm a firm believer in 'an eye for an eye', but you went too far with this, boy. I don't care who she is, or what games you're playing, killing our own was never part of the plan!"

"She's one of them! She was on the news! I saw her outside, and I remembered. I remembered, Master. You told me to take care of her. You told me not to do it myself. You told me to make it look like Parasupe so we wouldn't get in trouble for killing a human. No vampires were supposed to be on the dance floor when it happened. They weren't supposed to be there. It wasn't my fault."

"Not your fault that you compelled humans to shoot up my club? Not your fault that, when that didn't work, your fucked up thinking got three of my best vampires burned to ash? You were only supposed to follow him! You weren't supposed to interfere! Or, how about, instead of finally killing the woman as you were told, you had her tell her old company exactly where we are?" There was a deep sigh. "They'll be coming after us again. You know that." Another pause. "What the hell were you thinking, boy?"

"Parasupe killed my best friend. My brother." Jaz's voice rose to a whine. "I watched them cut him into tiny little pieces. And they would've done the same to me. They took my fang."

"Yes, they would have. You're lucky I found you when I did.

However, now that they know where we are, you may not be so lucky the second time around."

There was a brief pause. "He's fucking her, you know. He's fucking that Parasupe bitch. He wasn't going to kill her. And you're letting him get away with it, after what they did to us. He should die, too. He's not one of us!"

"Jaz, focus!" the master raised his voice before seeming to remember himself and lowering it again. "What on earth made you believe putting this coven on Parasupe's radar was a good idea?"

There was some shuffling around.

"Jaz!"

His next words burst from him like rushing water breaking through a dam. "So you would get rid of him! If it was his girlfriend that brought them here, it would be his fault for not letting her die when she was supposed to, for not killing her when you told him to. It's not my fault. It's Kohl's fault. You let him stay here! You let him stay here with us, even though he's a monster!"

"Kohl will be taken care of."

There was a few seconds of silence.

When Jaz next spoke, Hawke could hear the glee in his tone. "Master, I have the girl."

"What?" In his surprise, the Master forgot to keep his voice down.

"I have the girl. I brought her here for you."

"Show me." The Master's voice was edged with violence.

Hawke moved fast. In the brief moment it took them to come out of the room, he was already hidden behind the bar. Footsteps sounded, going in the opposite direction, and he heard the door to the caverns open and shut.

After a few seconds, he straightened to his full height, and poured himself another drink, his mind working furiously.

Pulling out his phone, he swiped the screen and started texting.

CHAPTER 20

Kohl got on his Harley. He only had about an hour before the sun came up. Margaret and her brother had refused to leave, and he'd spent most of the night trying to convince them otherwise. The pair of them quietly, but firmly, informed him they would not be chased from their home. Their parents worked their fingers to the bone building up the business after immigrating to the area so long ago, and they would not be abandoning it. They would take their chances. Nothing Kohl said would change their minds. All he could do was make them promise they'd hide in the shelter if need be and he would do all he could to protect them.

He pulled into The Caves thirty minutes later. The exposed skin on his face and hands prickled with warning of the coming dawn. For a brief moment, he seriously considered riding off into the sunrise and ending it there. Not because of what might be waiting for him inside, but because even if he survived this day, he would forever be alone from here on out. Being with Devon the last few days had shown him there was more possibility for him than he'd ever imagined. Even now, he could still feel the warmth of her in his arms. Could still see the specks of gold in her eyes. Smell her desire for him as they danced. Taste the potency of her blood and hear the sweetness of her cries when he was inside of her. She made him laugh, and she made him think. She made him feel like the male he wanted to be.

But it was all a ruse. He didn't know her at all.

As soon as he pulled around the back of the building, the hair on his arms and neck rose. All of the cars were gone and the club was closed up tight, lights off and doors locked. But that wasn't unusual given the hour.

No, something else was going on.

Letting himself in, he didn't hurry as he made his way down to the caverns to face the music. The Master was going to be angry with him for not obeying his command, but there was no way in hell he could bring himself to raise a hand to Devon, no matter what she'd done. And no matter how grateful he was for everything he'd done for him, the Master had another thing coming if he thought Kohl was just going to stand aside and allow him to send anyone to hurt her.

He didn't see a single soul as he made his way back to the throne room, and expected everyone to be gathered in the throne room. But when he got there, there was only one vampire present. Waiting.

The Master.

Their eyes clashed, and the dragon rumbled inside of him. Seems he wasn't the only one who was preparing for this confrontation.

The ancient vampire was silent as Kohl approached. The

back of his neck felt like it was on fire, but he resisted the urge to rub it away.

The Master cocked his head to the side. He looked older than the last time he'd seen him, but no less powerful. "Kohl."

Kohl lowered his eyes, but he did not kneel. His reprieve was over. It was time to face the music. "Master."

Rage radiated from the Master at his insolence, filling the room with icy fingers that clawed at Kohl's skin.

But the beast practically sang with anticipation.

The muscles in his jaw tensed but his tone was level as the Master asked, "Is the woman taken care of?"

Kohl drew himself up. "No. She's still alive. And I'm going to have to insist she stays that way." He didn't bother trying to defend himself, knowing the Master wouldn't want to hear it.

If he was surprised by Kohl's honesty, he didn't show it, although Kohl assumed he knew him well enough by now not to be surprised. There was no point in trying to lie or cover things up around a group of vampires. They might not be able to penetrate his thoughts on a whim, but they had other ways of finding out the truth.

The Master sat back on his throne and laced his fingers over his lean belly. "The woman is a danger to us and our kind. You were ordered to kill her, Kohl. Perhaps I didn't make myself clear."

"And I told *you* she was no threat to you or the coven."

"And yet, here I find myself, hiding in these caverns like a bat, because just a few hours ago a team of Parasupe assholes showed up to take us all out." His eyes drifted around the room. "I can't help but wonder how the fuck they found out about us? And how they just happened to know our exact location?"

Kohl remained silent. He couldn't defend her. Devon had as good as admitted to what she'd done. But that didn't mean he was going to hand her over, either.

The silence stretched on until the Master sighed dramatically and shrugged. "No matter now. The threat was severely undermanned for a coven of our size, and it has been taken care of. However, how many more are going to come now? I'm not going to spend another moment of my life running because you have a soft spot for a human."

The threat was severely undermanned...

The words went round and round in Kohl's head. He was right. A team of eight was nowhere near enough to attempt to take out an entire coven. It made no sense.

Perhaps, because they hadn't come here looking for an entire coven.

And suddenly it all clicked. Her confusion. The wisp of a scent in her hallway.

He was a fucking idiot.

Hoping his expression wouldn't give anything away, Kohl raised his eyes to meet the Master's mocking gaze. "Perhaps Jaz and his pals shouldn't have attacked her."

If he'd expected the Master to have a reaction to this statement, he was sadly mistaken. "Perhaps."

White-hot fury flared within Kohl. He bared his fangs, not bothering to hide his rage.

"As they haven't returned, am I to assume you used their bones for kindling for your fire?" The Master began to laugh, the sound slightly mad.

The Master's sharp eyes speared through him, perhaps sensing the dragon was just beneath the surface. At this moment, Kohl believed he would love nothing more than to breathe fire on the smug bastard perched on the throne before him like some sort of self-proclaimed god. But even after everything, something inside of him still balked at taking out the one who had given him a home and a family when he'd had nothing and no one. Squeezing his hands into fists, Kohl dropped his chin and reigned in the beast with some effort.

The laughter faded away. When Kohl raised his head again, the Master bared his fangs, pure hatred shining from his black eyes. He wasn't exactly sure what he'd done to deserve such wrath. And maybe he hadn't done anything. Maybe the Master had just never liked him because he was different, and more powerful, and therefore a threat.

Maybe the Master was just an asshole.

"You've tested me since the moment I allowed you into this coven, boy." He held up a hand when Kohl opened his mouth to protest. "Oh, you do as you're told, and you always seem willing to help out upstairs, but I sense your rebellious nature. All this time, you've been waiting…watching…to catch me at a weak moment."

"That's not true," Kohl protested, wondering where the hell this was coming from. "I've always been grateful for everything you've done for me and my mother."

The Master smiled. "Ah, yes. You're mother. She was a good woman, despite her filthy shifter blood. She knew her place, and she stayed in it. May she rest in peace." He made the sign of the cross, mocking a religion Kohl knew had brought nothing but destruction upon his people.

Then his black eyes landed on Kohl. A trace of uneasiness fluttered through his gut.

"Disobedience is not something I take lightly, Kohl. You must understand. If I allow you to get away with not following a direct order, I am opening the door for others to follow in your footsteps. I have held the position of Master of this coven for so long because vampires respect power, and power stems from strength, and from fear." His stare never wavered. "According to our laws, I have two options here."

Kohl pulled himself up to his full height. As long as Devon wasn't harmed, he would happily take on whatever punishment the Master saw fit to dole out.

"Banishment. Or death."

Whatever Kohl had been expecting, this was not it. "And which one is it going to be?"

The Master appeared genuinely conflicted. "I haven't decided. But until I do, get out of my sight."

Dismissed for the time being, Kohl turned on his heel and left the throne room, his head reeling. He knew there was no way he was getting out of there without the Master knowing about it and coming after him. He thought about trying to find Hawke, but he would only be dragging his friend into something he had no power over. If he tried to help Kohl, his life would also be on the line. He thought about finding Jaz, the dragon sharpening its talons eagerly, but it would only strengthen the case against him. No, if he wanted any chance of coming out of this alive, any chance to be with Devon, he needed to chill the fuck out.

In the end, he went back to his area of the caverns to wait out the Master's decision.

CHAPTER 21

Kohl awoke with a start, his heart pounding in his chest. Glancing down, he saw he was lying on top of his mattress, still in the same clothes he'd had on last night.

For a moment, he was disoriented. And then the events of the previous forty-eight hours crashed into his consciousness.

Devon.

Grabbing his phone off the nightstand, he checked for a text or a missed call. Nothing. If the time was right, and there was no reason it shouldn't be, he'd only slept a few hours. Which meant it was the middle of the day.

He laid the phone down beside him and went to get cleaned up. As he showered, he struggled with the urge to run back to his phone and call her. Or at least text. Maybe he should just take a ride by her place.

Sticking his face under the hot water, he admitted the truth to himself. He wanted to see her. He needed to see her. And not because he was thirsty. Because he missed her. He wondered if she'd actually left town, yet.

Soap stung his eyes.

Surely, that was it.

Kohl shut off the water and got dried off. He was being a fool. If he went after her now, he would be hunted like a boar, accused of running from his punishment. The Master wouldn't stop until he found him, and then he would be dead for sure.

Torn between what he knew he should do and what he wanted, Kohl walked back into his room and stared down at the phone for several long minutes.

Picking it up, he slid it into the back pocket of his jeans. He'd made his choice. And the Master would make his. Perhaps he'd get lucky and he'd only be kicked out of the coven. Then he'd be free to find Devon. He could put her on the back of his bike and they could ride away, and never look back.

Though unrealistic, it was a nice dream.

With a last look around to make sure he hadn't forgotten anything, he left his room and went in search of Hawke.

The rumble of a crowd came from the direction of the throne room, and though he wasn't quite ready to face the Master again, Kohl changed direction and headed that way.

Turning the corner, he frowned. Something major was going down, and as no one had bothered to come get him out of bed, he knew it had nothing to do with him. Still, Kohl approached the circle of vampires surrounding the Master's throne with some caution.

The crowd was restless, bloodlust thick as fog in the air. Hisses and growls of excitement echoed throughout the chamber, rising and falling with whatever was happening at the center of the circle. He saw the Master standing near his throne, his back to the crowd.

Kohl suddenly had a really bad feeling about this.

Hawke hovered toward the back of the crowd, and Kohl walked quietly up on his left side. The vibe in the room made him twitchy, and he hated to ask, worried this all had something to do with him and whatever outcome the Master had decided upon, but not knowing would be even worse. He kept his voice barely above a whisper, knowing Hawke would easily hear him. "What's going on?"

Hawke turned, startled. Glancing quickly around, he shoved Kohl's head down and walked him to the back of the cavern and around the corner, peering back over his shoulder to make sure no one had seen them. When they were out of sight, he released him. "What the fuck are you doing here?" Unlike the rest of the group, Hawke showed none of the signs of bloodlust. As always, he was calm and in control.

Kohl ran a hand through his hair, wondering that exact thing. "I came to see if I could talk to the Master. He gave me a choice this morning—death or banishment. Not my choice," he clarified. "His. If he was gonna kill me, he would've done it right then and there. Which I hope means he's leaning toward banishing me. But, this is my home. You're my family. I belong here with you."

"Why didn't you answer my text?"

"What text?"

"I texted you, Kohl. I tried to warn you not to come back here."

"I'm not gonna run, Hawke."

Hawke started to say something. Stopped. And then, with a resigned sigh, said, "Kohl. Devon is here."

The air punched out of his lungs and he suddenly forgot to breathe. No. That couldn't be. She was leaving. He'd seen it in her eyes. "That's not possible." Kohl stared at his friend, the only one he completely trusted in this place. Hawke would never lie to him.

The truth stared back at him. And it wasn't good.

A red haze blocked out their surroundings. His fangs shot down fast and hard, and he pulled his upper lip back in a snarl. "Where is she?"

Hawke nodded once toward the throne room. "In there." His hand gripped Kohl's arm in an iron vice before he could run back there. "But if you want any chance at all of staying with us, you can't interfere."

Kohl tried to pull away. Hawke's fingers dug into him. He dragged him further down the passageway. "Kohl! It's too late. You can't just waltz in there and take her. Not now."

"The fuck I can't."

"Kohl, the Master will rip your goddamn head clean off if you show up now."

"I'm not letting them hurt her, Hawke. You can stand with me on this, or you can take their side. I get it. Either way. I do. But I can't…" He closed his eyes tight as the dragon stretched its wings and released a menacing growl deep in its throat. The sound reverberated off the walls around them.

Hawke dropped his hand from his shoulder and took a step back, eyeing him warily.

Kohl opened his eyes. "I *won't* allow them to hurt her. She is *mine*."

Pacing away, Hawke covered his face with his hands. His voice was muffled behind them. "Aww, man. Please don't tell me you fed from her."

Kohl saw no reason to hide it anymore. "I did."

"Fuuuuuck, Kohl."

"I know." There was no excuse for it. He'd explicitly gone against the Master's direct order, adding to his list of crimes. "Jaz and a few others followed me the second night I saw her. He got a hold of her and bit her before I could get her back." He rubbed the back of his neck, trying to disperse the heat building there as he recounted what happened that night. "He fucking bit her. Claimed her. I couldn't allow it."

"Well, that explains how he found her again."

Kohl hissed, his fangs aching to tear into vampire flesh. "That's not how. I overrode his claim." He turned to go find Devon, and again, Hawke stopped him.

"You're sure you drank from her?"

What game was he playing? Kohl didn't have time for this shit. "I'm fucking positive, Hawke. She's mine."

Hawke gave him a strange look. "Then why didn't you know she was here?"

Kohl stilled as that truth slammed into him like an avalanche. He was right. He should've known she was here. He carried her blood. It should call to him like a fucking siren when they were this close and she was in trouble. Why hadn't he known she was here the moment he left his room? Or even before. "I've never claimed a female before." He paced back and forth in the narrow space, restless. "I felt her blood immediately after. Not so much a few hours later." And barely at all when he'd gone back to warn her. "Maybe it's just another thing that's fucked up about me."

"How do dragons claim their mates?"

His stomach rolled. "They burn them." Lifting his chin, he caught Hawke's look of disbelief.

"Holy fuck."

"Not all of her. Just…like a brand. Like cattle. Dragons

breathe in the ash of...the burn...and it embeds into the dragon and becomes a part of it. Something like that. Or, so my mother told me before she died."

"Well, why hasn't your beast stuck his name on her?"

Kohl pulled up short. "You're not fucking serious."

Hawke shrugged. "I'm just saying."

"She's only been around the dragon once. The night Jaz tried to take her. I started shifting as soon as I sensed they were there. I couldn't stop it." He thought of blowing fire on that perfect skin. "Besides, I don't think I could stomach doing that to her."

"Well, that's your choice. But I'm just thinking, if your beast —as you like to call it—laid claim to Devon...well, that sure as hell would make things interesting around here, wouldn't it?"

Kohl didn't have time to solve riddles. "I'm going after her, Hawke." His friend grabbed his arm and he shook it off. Baring his fangs, he hissed at him. "You can't fucking stop me. So, stop trying."

Hawke held both hands palms out in front of him. "I get it. You do what you have to do. But you need to know. She's not in good shape. I wasn't involved. She was like this when she was brought in."

He must've said something, made some sound, for Hawke backed farther away.

"One more thing I think you need to know. Because I have the distinct feeling only one of you is going to survive this night—either you or the Master. I wanted to tell you before now, but I didn't have the chance."

"What?" The word was barely understandable.

"It was Jaz. It was all Jaz. He's the one who recognized Devon the other night at the club. He's the one who mind fucked some humans into shooting up the place. He's the one who's been after her. And the Master knew about it the entire time. Though it did throw him off guard when Parasupe actually showed up here." Hawke grinned.

OVER THE COMMOTION of the vampires, a moan of pain came to Kohl's ears. It was so faint it was barely there, but Kohl knew instantly who it was. And it came from the throne room. With a last flash of his fangs, he bolted back down the passageway and barreled straight through the circle of hissing, hungry vampires, knocking them out of the way in his urgency to get to Devon.

In their trance of bloodlust, they sprang back up behind him and resumed their spots.

Devon sat within the center of the circle, tied to the throne like some kind of broken doll. She wore the same flannel pajama pants and T-shirt she'd had on when he'd left her, now soaked as red as her pants with blood. Her blood. Her hair cover was gone, and soft curls had escaped and stuck to her cheeks and forehead. Vampire bites covered her bare arms and neck. One leg of her pajama pants was ripped open to expose her inner thigh, and another bite was visible there.

The Master sat at her feet, leaning casually between her spread legs. When he spotted Kohl, he dropped the arm he'd been feeding from and smiled. "Ah! Look who's here. My ungrateful orphan."

He wasn't flouting Kohl's claim. He was killing her.

"I am not yours," Kohl growled. The dragon roared for release, and Kohl felt his skin crawl up his back. With a shiver of pure willpower, he controlled it. For the moment.

The Master launched himself forward, his hiss of displeasure raising the hair on the back of Kohl's forearms, the toes of his boots butting up against Kohl's, but Kohl held his ground.

Blood…Devon's blood…dripped down his chin and stained his blond hair. The dragon screeched with fury unlike anything Kohl had felt before. Sensors of heat chased each other across his skin as the dragon fought for freedom. Fighting the beast out of worry he'd hurt those he cared about, his line of vision narrowed until he only saw the vampire before him.

"I took you and your slut of a mother in when you had nowhere else to go. I gave you a roof over your head and humans to feed on. I protected you both. How dare you disrespect me! How dare you disobey me!" He threw his arm out, indicating the woman watching them through eyes that were no more than slits as she fought to stay conscious.

Kohl felt a shiver of fear. Not his own, but Devon's.

"You took this human as your own, after I ordered you not to!" He stuck a finger in Kohl's face. "Oh, yes. I know. Jaz saw it all. You broke the laws of the coven. And don't lie to me and tell me you didn't. Did you forget we have eyes everywhere? Even if we didn't, why else would you turn on your own kind? Why else would you refuse to kill her when she poses such a threat to those you claim to care about? And now—now!—you dare to dispute my claim on you?"

Kohl hissed a warning at the leader of their coven. He was making a scene because everyone was watching. His family—Kohl's family—was watching.

But the moment he saw her, spread before this room of vampires like some kind of sadistic buffet, Kohl knew he'd made the wrong choice. This was not his home.

Devon was his home.

He leaned down into the Master's face. "She is mine. You will release her to me. Right now. Or I will TAKE her." The warning was clear. He was challenging the Master. It was not something Kohl had ever planned, but he would do whatever he had to do to get Devon back. Even unleash the dragon on his own coven.

A brief look of uncertainty flickered across the Master's face. He knew damn well who would win this fight. But his black eyes never wavered, even as the crowd of vampires surrounding them roused from their feeding stupor and began to jostle each other with excitement over the chance to witness a fight for dominance, guaranteed to be long and bloody.

The Master bared his fangs in warning. "I don't think you want to go there, boy."

Kohl looked over the vampire's shoulder and met Devon's terrified eyes. The beast within calmed momentarily, and a fierce determination filled him as he tried to communicate to her it would all be all right.

A slight movement drew Kohl's attention back to the ancient vampire before him, and he smiled. "Oh, but I do." Lifting his wrist to his mouth, he bit through the skin until he tasted blood, tearing the vein open until it ran freely. He took a step back and tightened his fist, forcing the flow to drip onto the floor in a horizontal line between them. The tense silence filled the room as Kohl said loud and clear, "I challenge you as leader of this coven, *Master*."

Hisses and growls and the smacking sound of twenty vampires slapping their hands against their thighs in excitement erupted around them, but Kohl never took his attention from his opponent. There was no need to watch his back. The others wouldn't interfere. To do so would throw the fight and would be reason enough for the winner to remove hearts and put heads on pikes to make up for the shame they'd caused him. And no one would oppose it. It was a matter of honor.

The Master stared at him for a good five seconds. His left eye began to twitch.

Kohl knew well what he was feeling. He'd always been a docile member of the coven. So grateful to be taken in he never would have dreamed of so much as arguing with his Master, even though—despite Kohl's younger age—they both knew who was more powerful between them.

But Kohl had never wanted power. He'd never wanted to lead. Never wanted anything but to help as much as he could and live a quiet, unobtrusive life where no one outside of this coven would ever discover what he truly was.

That time was now over, unless he was willing to stand idly by while Devon was bled out until she was barely alive. He had no idea what the Master planned to do with her then—kill her or make her into one of his mindless slaves. But neither was an option that was acceptable to Kohl. Taking her away from him was the only way. And to do that, he would have to kill him. And to kill the Master meant he would, by blood law, be the new coven leader.

Kohl's heart fluttered in his chest and the room began to swim around him.

"Kohl."

His name. A whisper of a voice he thought he'd never hear again.

Everything came back into focus, and his heart stilled, hardening within his chest.

So be it.

Maniacal laughter erupted from the male before him. Throwing his head back, he spread his arms wide and laughed until the coven shifted restlessly behind Kohl, murmuring amongst themselves that perhaps he'd really lost his mind this time. Abruptly, he stopped, and brought his wrist to his mouth much the same way Kohl had. Squeezing his fist, he drew his own line in the dirt. He didn't say anything when he was finished, only stared at Kohl, daring him to cross it.

Kohl lowered his eyes to the overlapping lines of blood...

And stepped over them.

Without warning, the Master attacked, but Kohl was ready. Faster than the human eye could track, he sidestepped the first punch and landed his fist directly into the ancient vampire's kidney. It did little damage, but it sure as hell felt good.

The crowd of vampires hissed their approval.

All of the pent up aggression Kohl had suppressed over the years came boiling to the surface, and he quickly went on the offensive, landing punch after punch into the Master's face until his knuckles were raw and bleeding and his opponent was barely recognizable. But they healed almost as quickly as they busted open, and even if they didn't, it wouldn't have stopped him. He didn't use his fangs, even though they were aching to rip into flesh, only his fists. The brute force was a release, and kept the dragon restrained, but barely. Kohl shut everything out until he didn't even know who or what he was hitting. He didn't feel the shots the Master got in on him or the teeth sinking into his shoulder as his momentum took them both to the ground.

Suddenly, he was lifted and thrown through the air. Kohl landed on his back in the middle of the vampires, who'd parted when they saw him coming. It appeared the Master was finished being a punching bag. Springing to his feet, Kohl shook his head until his vision cleared. Balancing on the balls of his feet, he raised his fists and prepared to launch a new attack.

Before he was able to land a punch, Devon cried out. Kohl spun around, refocusing his rage on whoever was hurting her. He didn't need to see it to know something had happened. The dragon could feel her pain as though it were his own. But no one was near her.

The back of Kohl's neck was on *fucking* fire, his skin overly sensitive as the dragon screamed in rage and fought to be free. Distracted, Kohl ducked and pivoted just in time as the Master threw his arms out to capture him in a deadly bear hug. Diving into his legs, Kohl knocked him off balance, but he didn't fall.

Instead, he rose in the air until he hovered a good foot off the floor. His eyes were pure black, and his skin shimmered white. His fingers curled like claws as he pointed one at Kohl. "You're an idiot if you think anyone will follow someone like you!" His voice, at a normal volume to the others, filled Kohl's head until he wanted to slap his hands over his hears in an effort to block it out.

Kohl snarled his answer, thirsty for blood and ready to end it.

The Master curled his fingers into a fist, wrapping an invisible hand around Kohl's throat. Jaz came to stand behind him, as did most of the coven, blocking Devon from his view, and as Kohl struggled for air, he realized what the Master said was true. He would rather take the hit to his honor and win this fight any way he could rather than let a hybrid best him by brute force. And a good portion of the coven had no fucking issue with that.

Kohl stared at the man who'd protected and guided him for most of his life. He didn't struggle. It would be a waste of energy. He would never be able to break the grip of the invisible weight around his throat. His eyes began to water as he struggled to stay conscious, and for a moment, he panicked. But then slowly, tauntingly, the corners of his mouth turned up in a smile as he felt the dragon move restlessly inside of him.

Wanna come out and play?

The dragon screeched in response.

He had a brief instance of fear for Devon and Hawke, but then something happened that had never happened before. The beast was communicating with him, and he knew without a doubt Devon would be fine.

And hopefully, Hawke would have enough damn sense to get the hell out of the way.

His smile widened.

CHAPTER 22

Devon struggled against the rope binding her to the throne, but she was weak from the loss of so much blood and her muscles refused to function. Despite the sweat dripping down her temples and her spine, she was shivering with cold, and she had to fight to keep her eyes open. All her body wanted to do was sleep.

Her mind, however, was just fucking fine.

Vampires crowded in front of her, and she'd lost sight of Kohl what seemed like forever ago but was probably only a minute into the fight. The two vampires moved so fast, she couldn't tell who was winning anyway.

The crowd suddenly shifted restlessly, and a gap appeared. Through it, she could see Kohl's friend Hawke. He stood toward the back with a few others who were apparently either on Kohl's side or pleading the fifth. Whatever. Vampire politics meant nothing to her. She just wanted Kohl to survive this night. She wanted both of them to survive this night.

Hawke's face was completely expressionless, but his stance

was tense. Struggling to keep her eyes open, she screamed his name in her head, hoping like hell he would hear her. The fourth time she did it, she knew she'd succeeded when his eyes flicked over to her briefly before he went back to the fight.

She was gearing up to try again when she heard it.

Devon?

He didn't sound pleased with her, but she didn't give a rat's ass. *Oh, thank God. Help me, Hawke. Please.*

Slowly, his head turned in her direction. Devon knew she must look like some kind of bloody pagan offering, but she could only hope his stoic persona wasn't an act and he would be able to control the impulse to feed. She was gambling with her life, but she was running out of options here. *Please*, she begged him.

Kohl roared in anguish, or maybe it was anger, but she kept her focus on Hawke. *Please.*

His mouth twisted with something akin to annoyance as his eyes shot back and forth between her and Kohl.

Devon let out a sob of gratitude when he finally appeared in front of her on the dais. She didn't even see him move.

He assessed her injuries with cold, dark eyes. "I could heal you, but I don't think your boyfriend would like that." He pulled his upper lip back, showing her his fangs, extended and ready to feed. A shiver of fear slid up her spine as he leaned in and smelled her. "I can certainly see why my boy is so attracted to you, though." Shouts rose up behind Hawke, and he shifted his body to see what was going on, enough that Devon could see, too.

The dragon stared at her through Kohl's eyes. As she watched, he arched forward and two rows of spines tore through the skin and clothing along his back. Kohl raised his head, fangs bared as his focus shifted back and forth between her and Hawke. Horrible, heart-breaking sounds were ripped from his throat as the dragon fought its way out.

From the corner of her eye, Devon saw a group of vampires cautiously approaching Kohl with large, silver chains looped over their arms under the direction of the coven leader. The bastard laughed at Kohl, calling him horrible things, egging him on.

She turned back to Hawke, struggling against her bonds. "Please, hurry! We have to help him!"

But Hawke just gave her a knowing smile as he bent down to release her ankles first. "He doesn't need any help, honey. Trust me on this one." Once her legs were free, he moved up to her arms and body. "But we need to get the hell out of here, and fast, before he turns this place into an inferno."

With one arm around her waist, he helped her to her feet. Devon watched as the vampires threw the chains over Kohl as he struggled to shift. The weight drove him to his knees.

"Dammit. He's fighting it," Hawke said as he helped her down the step.

"Why? Why won't he save himself?"

"Because he's probably too worried about saving you."

The coven leader, floating a foot off the ground like some kind of possessed anti-Christ, lifted both arms over Kohl's body. The force of his will pushed Kohl all the way to the ground until he was nearly flat on his stomach. Devon had never seen or heard of anything like it. In all her years at Parasupe, she'd never run across anything stating vampires had this kind of power.

The crack of breaking bones reverberated around them.

Kohl's bones. And without thinking, Devon cried out to him. "Kohl!"

His head whipped around and he spotted her immediately. Glowing eyes narrowed in on Hawke's arm around her.

Hawke cursed under his breath as he propelled her toward the tunnel. "What the hell did you do that for?"

Three vampires suddenly appeared in front of them, halting their escape. Devon felt Hawke tense beside her.

"Where are you taking my dinner, Hawke?"

The coven leader's voice echoed in Devon's head. She winced in pain and pressed her free hand to the side of her head.

"Fuck. We're not getting out of here," Hawke said in her ear. "I'm so sorry."

Devon couldn't believe he was giving up so easily. "No. No! Just go around them."

"I can't. I'm sorry," he repeated.

Their bodies, still holding onto each other, began to turn. Devon looked down. Her feet weren't touching the ground, but were floating a few inches above it. She tried to reach for Hawke, tried to grip his shirt, but her arm wouldn't move. "What's happening?" But she knew exactly what was going on. Lifting her eyes, she saw the coven leader floating toward them. Behind him, Kohl lay sprawled on the ground beneath pounds of silver chains. Half vampire. Half dragon.

I never meant for all of this to happen. I never wanted to hurt you. I just wanted to be with you.

Devon focused on Kohl, trying to insert the words forcibly into his head with nothing but sheer willpower. She had no idea if he could hear her. He'd told her he couldn't communicate this way. But, still, she had to try.

He started to renew his struggles against the chains, and managed to lift his head. When he saw that she and Hawke had the coven leader's full attention, his face twisted into a mask of rage and he growled deep within his throat, baring his fangs. Devon watched in awe as he struggled to his hands and knees beneath the weight of the chains while the vampires on either side fought to keep him down.

Let him out, Kohl!

The coven leader floated closer, blocking her view, and the connection was broken.

The ground suddenly came up at her and Hawke and they landed hard. Devon found she could move again, and she did clutch Hawke's shirt this time.

Hawke spoke up. "Master, I was only trying to get her out of harm's way so you would—"

Hawke made a choking noise. Bending at the waist, his arm slipped from her as he attempted to draw air into his lungs. The coven leader's feet softly touched the ground and he strode toward them on legs like tree trunks enclosed in black leather. Blood streaked his blond hair and billowy white shirt. Her blood. And his own.

Devon's heart fought to continue beating as terror filled her veins with ice.

The coven leader stopped about six feet away. Cocking his head to the side, he watched Hawke struggle for breath. His face showed no remorse, no sign of emotion whatsoever.

They were going to die. They were all going to die.

The ice in Devon's blood suddenly turned to hope as two black, leathery wings spread to each side of the coven leader. She reached down and twisted her hand in the back of

Hawke's shirt, trying to pull him up and make him look. "Hawke! Look."

He raised his head, hauling in deep breaths as the coven master released his hold and looked over his shoulder.

The dragon rose up behind him. A great beast from some other time. Spreading his wings, he stretched his head toward them and released a scream that had chills chasing each other across her skin.

"Devon, you have to run!" Hawke wrapped his arm around her and pulled her away.

"He won't hurt me," she said.

"That may be true, but I don't know that he would have the same consideration for me. Let's go."

She let him lead her toward the tunnel, leaning her weight on him as vampires ran past them in blurs. After a few seconds, he bent down and swooped her up in his arms.

The air sucked at their backs as the dragon drew in a deep breath. Screams rent the air as the entire coven ran for their lives.

"Fucking hell, Kohl! Give me a minute!" Hawke shouted. He reached the passageway just in time and dodged around a piece of limestone that jutted out from the wall, ducking behind it just as a wave of heat pushed them to the ground, followed by a stream of fire.

Hawke slapped at the outside of Devon's thigh, and she belatedly realized she was on fire. Pushing his hands away before he set himself ablaze, she rolled away from him, smothering the flames in the dirt. Unfortunately, by doing so, she rolled right out into the middle of the tunnel. Her hair whipped around her face as Kohl drew in another breath, sucking the air from the enclosed space. Knowing she had to do something before he burned them all alive, even those he cared about, she rose up on her knees and held up her hands. "Kohl! Stop! Please, stop!"

The cavern was large enough for the dragon to stand. Multiple small, lingering fires burned around him filling the air with the stench of burnt hair and skin. About fourteen vampires, those who had been lucky enough to be behind the dragon when he torched the others, huddled in the back of the room, afraid to move for fear of drawing the beast's attention.

At the sound of her voice, his large head swung toward her, and a deep purr filled the room as he exhaled in plumes of smoke. Using the tips of his wings for leverage, he crawled toward her.

"Devon! What are you doing?"

She saw Hawke waving at her out of the corner of her eye, trying to get her to hide. "It's okay. He won't hurt me." Using the wall as leverage, she pushed herself to her feet and stumbled forward, away from Hawke's hiding place. Vampire or not, he had helped her, and for that, she owed him his life and would do whatever she could to distract Kohl's attention from him. Leaving the tunnel, she made it about twenty feet before her head began to swim and she lost her balance, falling onto her hands and knees.

Kohl "harmphd" in alarm and rushed toward her. Lowering his head, he nudged her with his nose.

"I'm all right," she said.

He didn't seem to believe her. He ran his nose over her, growling deep when he smelled the blood.

In her fifth or thirtieth attempt to get up, Devon fell to her side, exposing her burned leg.

When he came upon the scalded flesh, the dragon's large

body shuddered from head to tail. He snuffed at her burn, inhaling deeply. Carefully, he settled down beside her.

Devon touched the side of his neck, too weak to do much else.

Suddenly, the dragon's big body jerked and he grunted in pain.

The dragon lurched to his feet, and Devon saw the long cut in his belly dripping blood onto the ground. It looked deep. But there was no weapon anywhere, nothing that could have caused it.

Shoving her hair from her face, she searched for the source of his injury.

The coven leader stood in the center of the room with a wicked-looking knife in his hand, and he was smiling as he wiped the long blade on his leather pant leg.

Hawke appeared to her left. He, too, had his eyes on the coven leader, and apparently little regard for the danger he was putting himself in. He looked around at the burning bodies of those vampires who hadn't gotten out of the way in time. Anger twisted his features. With fangs bared in warning, he hissed. "This is your fault, *Master*. You shouldn't have brought her here! Look what you've done."

"I didn't bring her here. Jaz did. On my orders," he added with a smirk. He glanced at one of the burning bodies. "Loyal until death, that one."

The dragon wrapped his tail around Devon, pulling her close to him.

She looked up just in time to see his sides expand as he opened his jaws and pulled in a breath.

Focused on the coven leader, Hawke didn't even notice.

The vampires at the back of the room, now in the direct line of fire, began to scatter.

Devon shoved at Kohl's side to get his attention, giving them time to get to safety. She didn't know if these vampires were good or bad, but they deserved a chance to save themselves.

One eye focused on her, then on Hawke, then on the others edging toward the tunnels, and she saw a spark of comprehension. Releasing Devon from the curve of his tail, he began to flap his wings, deep gusts of air knocking Hawke and the other vampires still in the room off their feet. With a running start, he rose into the air, and Devon watched in disbelief as he captured the coven leader, catching him off guard. Holding him gripped in one talon, he flew up into the smooth ceiling above. He slammed into it with his muscular back, over and over, until he started busting through the limestone.

The coven leader struggled to get free, but with his arms trapped at his sides, there was little he could do.

The ceiling began to crumble down around them. Devon suddenly found herself in Hawke's arms, rushing back toward the tunnel. They made it just as the dragon broke through, and a large piece came crashing back down to the ground. Sunlight streamed down through the hole he'd created, glinting off the rippling jewel tones of his dark scales.

Terror ripped through her and Devon screamed, certain he'd burn alive right before her eyes. She tried to run to him, but Hawke held her back.

"It's okay, Devon." He was annoyingly calm. "Watch."

Kohl flapped his enormous wings and flew up and out of the caverns, the Master still gripped in his talon. But as soon as the sun's rays hit the vampire, he burst into flames, disintegrating into dust and ash that floated down through the beams of sunshine like fairy dust, until it gently touched down on the cavern floor.

Catching a gust of wind, the dragon flew higher and higher toward the sun.

Devon watched him until he was only as large as a bird.

And then he was gone.

CHAPTER 23

That night, Kohl rushed down the ramp and through the caverns. "Hawke! Hawke! Goddammit, where are you?"

Per the dragon's usual drill, he'd woken up in the center of the field near the restaurant. This time, he'd managed to remain conscious while shifting back, and barely made it to the back door in time. He'd busted inside, breaking the hinges, and threw his naked ass into the center of the room, slapping at his smoking skin.

Nonplussed, Margaret had turned from the stove and threw a large pot of lukewarm water over him she'd just set to boil, while her brother ignored him completely and opened one of the ovens to check on whatever was cooking inside.

After promising to pay to have their door fixed, he'd spent the remainder of the afternoon below ground, pacing a hole in the carpet. Using Margaret's phone, he'd tried to contact Devon, Hawke, and Andrew, but no one was picking up. He'd contemplated sending someone over to check on things, but immediately discarded the idea. It was too dangerous. Finally, he'd settled down enough to shower and dress, but he didn't get any sleep that day.

"Hawke!" He came upon the throne room and skidded to a stop. The entire coven was there, cleaning up piles of rubble in the middle of the room. Confused, he drew a breath to call out to Hawke again, and smelled fresh air. Slowly, his eyes travelled upward. There was a giant hole in the ceiling of the cavern.

Large enough for a dragon to fly through. "Holy fuck."

Andrew was the first to notice him standing there, and he immediately dropped the large rock in his hands and dropped to one knee. He slapped the guy next to him on the leg, who frowned at first, but upon seeing Kohl, immediately did the same. It continued with a domino effect until the entire room was silently kneeling before him.

Kohl's eyes swept the room, but he didn't see Hawke. Or the Master. A sense of foreboding had the room spinning around him. "Where is Hawke?" he asked Andrew. He would never forgive himself if he had hurt his friend in any way. It didn't matter that he retained no memories when he became the beast.

Andrew lifted his head and pointed back down the tunnel, toward Kohl's rooms. "He's in your room. With the woman."

"Devon?"

"Yeah."

"Thank you." Kohl spun on his heel, glancing back only once. Questions spun around in his head, but right now he only needed one answer.

Halfway to his room, Devon's scent came to him, along with Hawke's. He realized with a start that the growl he heard was coming from him. And his fangs were bared. Kohl gave himself a hard shake. Hawke was his friend. There was no reason to act this way. The dragon disagreed, but they could argue about it later.

He wasn't prepared for the sight that met him when he got to his room.

Devon was curled up on his bed with her back to him. She wore one of his T-shirts and what looked like little else. Her beautiful golden-brown skin was ashen, and there was an ugly burn in the shape of a misshapen star covering the outer portion of her right thigh.

Hawke sat in the chair near the bed with his elbows on his knees and his fingers pressed together, staring at the floor.

Kohl must have moved or said something, for suddenly Hawke's head snapped up and he leapt to his feet. It was proof of his distraction that he hadn't noticed Kohl was there before then. "Are you all right?"

But Kohl couldn't take his eyes from the scalded flesh on Devon's leg. "Did I do that?" A fever raged inside of him, burning so hot his eyes watered and he could barely see. "Hawke? Did I fucking do that to her?"

Hawke said nothing.

Kohl fell back into the wall behind him, pressing the heels of his hands against his eyes to block out the sight.

A heavy hand fell on his shoulder. "She needs you. Kohl! You gotta snap out of it. Devon needs your blood or she isn't going to make it."

Kohl swallowed hard and pulled his hands away from his face. "I'm no good for her."

"Forget all that for right now, man. You can save her."

"Why didn't you do it?" The instinct to claim her had him baring his fangs even as he made the suggestion.

"And have my best friend come in here and rip my head off the moment he smelled my blood inside of her? Or worse?" Hawke laughed without humor. "No thanks."

"I wouldn't have done that."

"Ha! Who the hell do you think you're fooling? This is me you're talking to. And this girl is yours, whether you like that idea or not."

Oh, he liked the idea. He liked it a whole hell of a lot. But... "So you were just gonna let her die? What if I didn't come back?"

"Then I would have saved her. Of course." Hawke slapped him on the shoulder. "What the hell are you standing here arguing with me for? Go do your thing. I'll leave you two alone. We'll talk after you've dealt with this."

"With her," Kohl said.

"What?"

"With *her*," he repeated. "She's not some...situation to be dealt with. She's smart and she's strong and she's important to me."

Hawke gave him a grim smile. "I know she is. That's why I risked my ass to help her." He picked up his jacket from the end of the bed. "Come find me when *Devon* is doing better."

After he left, Kohl went to her, sitting carefully on the edge of the bed. "Dev. Wake up, honey." He brushed her hair back off her face. "Come on. Don't do this to me. Wake up, Devon."

Her eyelids twitched, then blinked open. She stared at the wall for a few seconds, then slowly turned her head. A smile turned up the corners of her colorless lips. "Hey. You're back. And you're okay."

The woman was half alive and *she* was worried about *him*. He released the breath he hadn't realized he'd been holding, bent over, and pressed a lingering kiss to her forehead. Relief flooded through him. Relief so overwhelming, for a few seconds he thought he was going to end up passed out beside her. "I need to ask you something," he whispered against her soft skin. It was cool and clammy to his lips.

"What's that?"

Kohl sat up just enough so he could focus on her face, not quite believing he was doing this after everything that had happened, but knowing it was the right thing to do. She deserved to have a choice. He glanced down at the visible bite marks on her arms, glad to see Hawke had washed away most of the blood.

"Kohl?"

He met her tired eyes.

"What did you want to ask me?"

She tried to roll over onto her back, and he scooted over a bit to give her some room, then took her hand between both of his. Bringing it to his mouth, he kissed her fingertips. "I need to ask you what you want me to do." Words caught in his throat, but he forced them out. "I can take you to a human hospital right now. They'll be able to help you there. Give you blood. Treat your burn. And you'll be okay. I can drop you off there and then go get Frank to come stay with you."

"And what about you? Where would you go? What's going to happen with your coven?"

"I don't know," he told her honestly. "But you would be safe and healthy, and that's all that really matters to me." He felt her eyes on him, but he kept his own focused on her hand, so slender and humanly fragile between his own.

"And I wouldn't see you again," she deduced.

"No, probably not. If that's what you wanted."

"And what's my other choice?" Her voice broke, and she coughed. "What's the other choice, Kohl?"

He did look at her then, and he didn't try to hide from her. Instead, he allowed everything he was feeling in that moment to show through on his face. All of the hope. The longing. The wanting. The dragon stirred deep within, and Kohl didn't fight it. She needed to see it, too, so she would fully understand what she would be agreeing to. "You can stay here with me, and I can give you my blood. It will heal you. It will more than heal you."

"And I will stay with you? After?"

He gave her a nod. "And you'll stay with me."

"For how long?"

Forever, he wanted to say. "For as long as you'll have me."

Little lines appeared between her brows. "And what about you?"

"Me?"

"Who will you be with?"

For a second, he was completely fucking confused, but then it came to him. She wanted to know if he would be faithful to her. "Dev, I haven't been with anyone since I met you that night upstairs. Not for sex, or to feed. And it would stay that way."

"So, basically, you would depend on me for everything."

"Yes."

"And why would you want to put yourself in that position?" A smile teased the corners of her mouth.

"Because I want you," he told her in all seriousness. "I think you're smart, and beautiful, and way too fucking good for me. But all I want right now is to be near you. All the time. Every damn day. I listen for the sound of your voice everywhere I go.

The littlest things remind me of your scent. I want to sleep beside you. I want to have deep conversations with you about God and souls, and silly ones about the latest show you and Frank are binge watching. I want to hear you laugh, and figure out what makes you tick. I want to build that house, and watch you lay out by the lake, soaking up the warmth of the sun. And at night, I want to drink the sunlight in your skin. I want to share my life with you." He paused to draw a breath.

"Kohl?"

"Yeah?"

"Why are you still talking? I'm dying here and you're blathering on and on...."

Laughter rumbled in his throat.

Devon rubbed his beard with her fingertips and then laid her palm against the side of his face. "I want to be with you, Kohl. I want all of that stuff you just said."

Turning his face, he kissed the center of her palm. "Are you sure? This life isn't what you're used to."

"So, you'll teach me how to mix drinks," she said.

"That's not what I meant."

"Kohl. I want you. I want to be with you." Her hand slid down the front of his shirt until it rested over his heart. "But what about the other side of you? What does he think about all of this?"

"He's already laid his claim, it seems." With his thumb, he skimmed the outer edges of her burn.

She frowned up at him. "The burn? Are you serious? I thought it was an accident."

Kohl nodded. "It's how dragons mark their mates, from what I've been told."

"Then why are we even discussing this? Pour me a drink."

He only hesitated a brief second before he lifted his wrist to his mouth and bit through the skin until he tasted blood, then he lifted her head with his other hand and held it to her mouth.

Unlike him, Devon didn't hesitate at all. The moment she tasted his blood, she groaned with pleasure and settled in to drink. When the wound began to heal itself, she wrapped her hands around his arms and bit down hard, her eyes flashing up to his when he grunted. But she didn't stop.

His upper lip lifted, exposing his fangs as her pleasure roared through him.

Her bites began to heal. Slowly, at first. And then all at once. He allowed her to drink until not a trace of the wounds remained. Shifting his hips away from her leg, he studied her burn. The blistered and damaged skin was now a bright pink. Over time, it would dull, but the scar would remain.

The mood in the room suddenly shifted, and Kohl's head snapped up. Her eyes, so dull and lifeless just a few moments ago, burned with golden fire. Strength filled her hands where they clenched around his arm, holding his wrist to her mouth. She began to move restlessly on the bed, rubbing her thighs together and arching her back.

Kohl pulled his wrist away despite her sounds of protest and licked the bite clean. Fire raged through his blood and his dick was so hard it felt like it was about to explode. He needed to touch her. He needed to be inside of her.

Rising from the bed, he quickly shed his clothing. Devon tried to follow his lead, but he moved so fast she barely had a chance to sit up before he was helping her. With mixed feelings of relief and impatience, he saw she still wore her underthings. Kohl made quick work of them, practically tearing the strips of lace and cotton from her body.

His mouth came down hard on hers. He tasted the blood on her lips—his blood—and he growled with hunger as he pressed her down upon the mattress. Devon lifted her hips to meet him, fingers clawing at his back, making those little sounds he loved so much.

Sliding one arm beneath her leg, he opened her to him, and with one smooth thrust, he slid inside her wet heat. Kohl rolled his hips, pushing deeper still. Her body stretched to fit him, clenching around him as he withdrew only to thrust again.

Devon met him each time, her moans mixing with his. The fullness of her breasts taunted him, and Kohl bent his head to catch one stiff dusky-brown nipple in his mouth. His throat burning with thirst, he couldn't resist nipping through her skin just enough for a taste of the sweet blood running just below the surface. Devon held his head to her breast as he suckled her, welcoming his ever-increasing thrusts.

And it still wasn't enough.

Her blood called to him, and Kohl raised his head. Their eyes clashed. His burning. Hers heavy-lidded with passion. Kohl bared his fangs, breathing in her scent. He didn't say anything. He didn't have to.

"I want you," she said, and then she exposed her neck to his hungry gaze.

Blood pulsed in time to her racing heart, taunting him, and Kohl sank his fangs into her throat with a moan of pleasure. Her blood rushed into his mouth. Feeding him. Nourishing him. Re-energizing him. It travelled through his body with the force of a freight train, stimulating every cell and every muscle, flowing through him until his head felt like it was going to float off his body and his dick swelled painfully.

The beast stretched, filling his limbs until he was the

dragon and the dragon was him. Both of them loving Devon as she whimpered with need, her fingers digging into his arms, hanging on as she reached her climax and her body convulsed beneath him, squeezing him until he felt his own release hit the base of his spine, barreling up his cock and into her sweet heat. Releasing her from his bite, Kohl rose above her and threw his head back, his hips pumping uncontrollably until he couldn't give her anymore.

When it was over, he fell on top of her, his body shuddering with the after effects. When he felt he could move, he rolled off of her and pulled her up against his side.

They lay like that until they caught their breath, fingers lazily touching warm skin, until Devon broke the silence. "So, what happens now?"

He kissed the curls on her temple. "I have no fucking idea."

EPILOGUE

Kohl sat at the bar inside The Caves and watched Devon in the center of the dance floor, wearing an airy red dress and red shoes. Her hair floated around her face, reminding him of the first time he saw her here. Only this time, she wasn't hiding in the dark. And she wasn't alone. Frank, her "BFF" danced with her. They were the only two on the floor. The club didn't open for another thirty minutes.

Music pulsed through his blood in time to the seductive movement of her hips. He loved to watch her lose herself to the music. It was the only time she was really free. He understood the feeling flowing between them. It was how he felt when he flew under the stars.

Now that he was more accepting of his "other half", as Devon liked to call it, Kohl was working on his relationship with the beast inside of him, and they were finding a way to coexist. Of course, this meant there was three of them during intimate moments. Devon didn't seem to mind. She didn't view the beast as something other, but rather just another part of him.

And Kohl was learning she was right.

Once he'd accepted this, he was finding it easier and easier to share in the dragon's experiences as well, which meant there were times he got to enjoy basking in the sun, and the freedom of flying.

Someone jostled his arm and he tore his eyes away from the erotic sight on the dance floor with obvious reluctance.

Hawke settled onto the stool next to him. "Hey, man."

Kohl took a sip of his beer. "Hey."

"How's the house coming?"

Kohl thought about the home he was building for him and Devon—lakefront property, with a windowless first floor and a large second story deck. He'd also contracted for special windows upstairs, so he could watch her lay out in the sun in nothing but bikini bottoms. "Good. It should be ready just in time for summer."

"That's good."

Kohl searched his friend's face. He hadn't come up here for idle talk. "Something else going on?"

Hawke waved hello to Devon, and she smiled back. "Now that things have settled down, we need to talk about the future of this coven."

"Hawke, I already told you. I'm not cut out for that shit. And I don't deserve it. Not after what I did to Jaz." Sorrow filled him. In his mind, Jaz had been a victim in all of this as much as Devon was.

"Knock it off," Hawke told him. "Jaz knew what he was doing. He was out for revenge. For the most part, the Master just told him how to do it. As far as I'm concerned, Jaz got what was coming to him." He took a long drink of his vodka. "You challenged the Master, and won. The role of coven leader is now yours. No one will challenge it."

"Not even you?" Kohl had wanted to ask that question for a while now, but up until now, he'd always hesitated. He wasn't sure why.

Hawke met his questioning stare. "Not even me."

"That's not right. You should be the next coven leader. You're older, and you were the Master's right-hand man. The others will follow you without question. And I don't even remember half the fight."

"There's no question now, Kohl. They're too fucking scared of you."

"That doesn't make me feel better."

"It is what it is." Hawke gave him a tight smile. "We need to make it official. Soon. Also," he continued before Kohl had the chance to protest more. "I've been thinking. Since it appears you're planning to keep her around for awhile, I think we should put Devon's skills to use."

Since he was the one who'd brought up that idea to begin with, Kohl tried to contain his sarcasm. It didn't really work. "*You've* decided."

Hawke grinned.

The song ended and Devon came over and grabbed Kohl's beer while Frank headed toward the restroom. "What's up, Hawke?"

"Not much, beautiful." He winked when Kohl flashed his fangs and quite obviously pulled her closer to him. "At least he's not hissing at me, anymore," Hawke told her.

"You could just stop saying stuff you know will bring out my worst side," Kohl suggested.

"I could," Hawke agreed. "But why the hell would I when it's so much more fun to rile you up?"

Devon held up her hands. "All right, guys. Put your penises back in your pants."

Kohl gave Hawke a warning look. "Don't say it, man. Just don't."

Hawke held up both hands in a gesture of peace. Walking behind the bar, he helped himself to a bottle of vodka. "Actually, Devon, we were just talking about you."

"About me? Why?"

"We think it's time you made yourself useful around here."

"We were going to *ask* you," Kohl corrected. "For your help."

"What kind of help?"

Hawke rested his hip on the counter behind him. "We want you to make use of your hacking skills."

She turned to Kohl. "I don't know if that's such a good idea after what happened last time."

"That wasn't your fault, Dev. And you know it." Kohl exchanged a look with Hawke, who gave him a nod. He turned back to Devon. "But I hope you remember how you did it. We want you to help us take out Parasupe."

Taking another swig of his beer, she stared at him over the top of the bottle, then wiped her mouth on the back of her hand. She looked back and forth between the two vampires.

"Then we're gonna need some help."

The door opened and a woman with red hair came in the main entrance. She hesitated once she was inside, blinking as her eyes adjusted to the dim lighting. Looking around, she spotted the three of them at the bar, but made no move to come forward.

"I'll go tell her we're not open yet," Kohl said as he stood. But Hawke stopped him with a hand on his arm.

"No. I've got this."

Kohl glanced back to find his friend's eyes firmly affixed on the woman. "Are you sure?"

Hawke gave him a nod, his attention never wavering from the stranger at the edge of the dance floor. Running his fingers through his dark hair, he stood and approached her.

She watched him come, a smile teasing her lips.

ABOUT THE AUTHOR

L.E. Wilson writes Paranormal Romance with Bite (because Vampires!) starring intense alpha males and the women who are fearless enough to tame them — for the most part anyway. ;) In her novels you'll find smoking hot scenes, a touch of suspense, a bit of gore, and multifaceted characters, all working together to combine her lifelong obsession with the paranormal and her love of romance.

Her writing career came about the usual way: on a dare from her loving husband to "write a damn book" already while folding laundry one day in Texas. Taking that as the challenge that it was, she grabbed her mango Hard Lemonade, hit the pool, and Blood Hunger, the first book of her Deathless Night Series, was born. Little did she know just one casual suggestion would open a box of worms (or words as the case may be) that would forever change her life.

Peach tea and her tiara are a necessary part of her writing process, though sometimes you'll find her typing away at her favorite Starbucks. She walks two miles to get there, to make up for all of those coffees. On the weekends she likes to hike, garden, cook vegan food, and have date nights with her favorite guy.

On a Personal Note:
"I love to hear from my readers! Contact me anytime at le@lewilsonauthor.com."

Keep In Touch With L.E.
lewilsonauthor.com
le@lewilsonauthor.com

Made in the USA
San Bernardino, CA
03 September 2018